SUPERDREADNOUGHT 4

SUPERDREADNOUGHT 4

SUPERDREADNOUGHT™ BOOK FOUR

CH GIDEON   CRAIG MARTELLE   TIM MARQUITZ
MICHAEL ANDERLE

We can't write without those who support us
On the home front, we thank you for being there for us

We wouldn't be able to do this for a living if it weren't for our
readers
We thank you for reading our books

Craig Martelle Social

Website & Newsletter:
http://www.craigmartelle.com

Facebook:
https://www.facebook.com/AuthorCraigMartelle/

Michael Anderle Social

Website: http://www.lmbpn.com

Email List: https://lmbpn.com/email/
Facebook:
https://www.
facebook.com/TheKurtherianGambitBooks/

SUPERDREADNOUGHT 4 TEAM

Thanks to our Beta Readers

James Caplan
Kelly O'Donnell
Micky Cocker
John Ashmore

Thanks to the JIT Readers

Peter Manis
Jackey Hankard-Brodie
Misty Roa
Diane L. Smith
Micky Cocker
Mary Morris
John Ashmore
Jeff Eaton

If I've missed anyone, please let me know!

Editor
Lynne Stiegler

CHAPTER ONE

Muultar. Another planet in a system that had meant nothing a year ago.

The captain's new body looked real. Felt real. Responded the way the AI known as Reynolds thought a human body would respond. He ran on the treadmill, accelerating to fantastic speed before leaping forward, executing a double flip, and landing on his feet.

"Looks like systems are nominal," Takal, the professor who designed and built the body stated without having watched the android. He checked boxes and made digital marks on his datapad. "What is the new Reynolds going to do?"

"Management by walking around," Reynolds replied, straightening his custom uniform and flicking a speck of lint off his sleeve. "Things are coming together. I need to show the meatbags that I'm here for them."

"I suggest you don't call the living beings 'meatbags,'" Geroux offered from her position behind a wall of computer screens.

"I've been told that before, but you are. I mean no offense. When people yell, 'Hey, android' at me, I don't think less of them for stating the obvious. I think I shall work on my ability to growl and swear as I've seen human leaders do in the movies from Earth. I'm torn between executive me and dashing, devil-may-care me. I shall embrace my hard side until further notice."

"Of course. I shall follow your new personality as it's interesting how you can turn things on and off. We aren't as evolved as you," Takal told him graciously. "If you'll allow *us* our foibles, you'll realize an improvement in how people see you, dashing or not."

"Thank you," Reynolds replied. He watched Takal's face, but the old Larian gave nothing away. He was already embroiled in a different project. "Prepare to go ashore. I think we'll need you on Muultar."

"Hmmm?" Takal mumbled. "What's there?"

Reynolds was already on his way out the door, and he didn't bother to answer. He had no idea, but thought it best if his key staff was prepared to deploy at all times. He chuckled as he walked away, thinking about the cult lackey from Muultar. He was finally on a trail that could lead him to the last surviving Kurtherians. The puzzle pieces that made up his mission were falling into place.

He ran into three crewmen from three different races working on a bank of conduits running along a corridor. A maintenance bot was directing their actions. One of the crew shot to attention, and the other two followed. Something fell, then one of the lines arced. "Bastard!" the shortest exclaimed as she jumped out from under the shower of sparks. The bot sprayed fire retardant on the conduit and started guiding the crew through repairing their repairs.

The AI hadn't said a word, but he'd had an impact on the crew. Not the one he was going for, however. Since Reynolds was the ship, he knew the line's systems were bypassed, and there was no impact to the superdreadnought's functionality. He left the crew to their task and headed for the elevator.

Maybe I'll just go to the bridge.

Ensign Ria Alcott brought the SD *Reynolds* through the Gate into the Quadrain system, shields up, weapons armed, and at a safe distance from nearby planets to avoid stumbling into anything.

"Lesson learned, sir!" she called, grinning. "We're here safe and sound."

"Don't dislocate your shoulder patting yourself on the back just yet," Tactical told her.

"He's right, although it bothers me to admit it," XO said. "That Loranian ship could be anywhere."

"That's not our biggest problem right now," Asya announced.

"We step into another firefight?" General Maddox asked, even though the tactical display showed no hostile targets.

"No!" Ria shot back.

"No," Asya assured him. "More like an asteroid field."

She brought up the view outside the ship, showing chunks of debris flying everywhere. "This system looks as if it's pissed off. Those three suns are beating up the place. Can't say it's tourist-friendly."

"Radiation levels are off the charts, too," XO called. "The gravitic shields are keeping us safe for now, plus our standard rad-shields, but if we're sticking around for a while, we're going to want to look into reinforcing our defenses."

"I'm not interested in looking like that burnt-toast cultist and his Muultu buddies," Tactical complained.

"Not much chance of that," Jiya told him, her gaze inadvertently going to Reynolds as he strolled onto the bridge.

With his new faux-flesh, his android body might not be so lucky.

She found it strange to look at him now after having seen his evolution from the Jonny-Taxi body she'd help steal for him to the older construct Takal had pieced together to maintain the AI's *essence* without degrading.

The new body looked so human that it caught Jiya off-guard every time she saw it. If it weren't for the AI's mannerisms and the crass, cutting sarcasm that was so much a part of Reynolds, Jiya would have had a hard time reconciling the new body with the Federation AI.

Had she passed him on the street, she would never have known he was an Android.

Even knowing, it still caused a hitch in her brain.

He walked so casually now, and so gracefully. There was none of the stutter of parts breaking down or the creak of damaged metal joints. For all intents and purposes, he was as human as any of them.

Well, more so, she thought, chuckling to herself, *seeing as how none of us are human.*

Alive *would be a better word,* she corrected herself.

"Get Takal up here to examine these radiation readings," Reynolds ordered. "Let's see if he can come up with something since I have no idea how long we'll be here. Better safe than sorry."

If the Phraim-'Eh cultists are here, we'll stay as long as it takes to root them out, Jiya thought.

A rumbling vibration pulled her out of her internal discourse, and she glanced at the viewscreen.

"I'm moving us to the edge of the asteroid field," Ensign Alcott reported, but the scrunched expression on her face suggested it wasn't as easy a task as she had hoped it would be.

"What edge?" Tactical asked. "This whole system is one big clusterduck of floating debris."

"Scanners show there were seven planets here not long ago," Comm reported. "There are only four now, which explains the mess."

"The planets in the Goldilocks Zone have avoided being torn apart, and one other," XO stated.

"I'm thinking this porridge is still too fucking hot," Tactical muttered.

"I agree," Reynolds said. "Muultar is skirting the edge of the habitable zone. Another hundred thousand years or so and it will be floating rocks like the rest of its neighbors."

"If that long," XO said. "The debris is pelting the planets, on top of the increased radiation. A big enough chunk hits it, and—"

"Say goodbye to the dinosaurs." Tactical laughed.

"Dino-what?" Jiya asked, wondering what Tactical was talking about.

Reynolds waved off the question. "Just get us as far away from the wreckage as possible, Ensign," he ordered. "We can better examine the system if we're not being peppered by debris."

The superdreadnought eased out of the asteroid field as gracefully as possible, but it was slow going. The shields flashed as they deflected a number of impacts before Ria managed to get them mostly clear.

The majority of the field hurtled beneath them, its passage playing across the viewscreen.

"Best I can do, sir," Ria called.

"It'll have to do," Reynolds answered. "Bring up the long-range scanners and give me a detailed report on the system. Get me as much information as you can about Muultar. I want to know what we're walking into."

Jiya bit back a sigh at Reynolds' subtle dig at their recent performance.

Their last mission had started off on the wrong foot. As capable as the crew were, and however naturally talented at stepping into their roles and doing a good job, they weren't as well-trained as they should be.

Too few of the crew had real military training or experience, and those who did—specifically General Maddox and Captain Asya—were handicapped by the rest of the crew's ignorance.

Jiya could only imagine how difficult it was for Asya and Maddox to keep up with everything, factoring in all the outcomes and likely consequences for every order given.

It was impossible.

Despite what they'd done together and all they'd accomplished, the crew was new, and they were learning on the job. Mistakes were bound to happen, but Jiya was determined to limit those as best she could—especially her own.

As first officer, she had recently instituted mandatory training sessions for all hands. With the help of Reynolds' other personalities, they had arranged for crash courses on everyone's role on the ship, including primary and secondary tasks.

She'd mandated a minimum of two hours a day for training, and had strongly *suggested* that the crew take advantage of every additional moment to interface with the ship in order to better understand their place aboard it.

They were tired and perhaps a little stressed, but Jiya could spot the advances they'd made. The crew seemed surer of themselves and more confident.

That was how *she* felt.

"I'm picking up motion in the asteroid field," Maddox announced.

"Hence the reason they're called asteroids," Tactical shot back.

Maddox scoffed. "I'm not talking about rocks, Tactical. We've got company."

"Want me to hail?" Comm asked.

"Not yet. What have you got, Maddox?" Reynolds asked.

"Two...no, three signals incoming," the general answered. "They appear to be small craft, slightly larger than our Pods. There's no evidence of weaponry. They're not fighters."

"And they're headed our way?" Reynolds questioned.

"Not directly," Maddox replied. "They seem to be skimming the surface of the asteroids as they flit around inside the field. It's like they're looking for something."

"But not us, right?" Jiya asked.

Maddox shook his head. "No, doesn't look that way."

As Maddox zeroed in on the ships so they showed on the viewscreen, one of the small craft landed on the flat surface of an asteroid and latched on.

"What the hell are they doing?" XO wondered.

There was a quick spark at the base of the oddly-shaped craft, then a cloud of dust rose up around the ship. It floated into space and obscured their view.

"Get me a closeup of that ship," Reynolds ordered as the other two landed on different asteroids and began the same process.

Maddox zoomed in, but if he understood what was being done, he didn't say anything.

Takal walked onto the bridge then, the door hissing shut behind him. He strolled over to where Reynolds stood and *humphed*.

"I wonder what they're mining?" he said casually.

The whole crew turned to look at him.

He shrank under their sudden glares. "What?" He brushed his chin. "Do I have crumbs in my beard?"

"You think they're mining?" Reynolds questioned.

"Oh." Takal chuckled, leaving his beard be. "Yes, I'm certain of it, although I have no idea what they're attempting to extract."

He gestured to the alien ship, which had a small front section where Jiya presumed the pilot sat, and a large, boxy back section that could accommodate bulk storage.

"I've seen ships similar to these," Takal went on. "There are excavation devices arrayed across the bottom of the craft. Numerous mechanical arms dig into the surface while several others sort the useful minerals from the debris and load them into the ship for conveyance."

"To Muultar, I presume," Reynolds said.

Takal shrugged. "Most likely, given the choice of habitable planets in the system." He gestured to the screen.

"Any indication the ships know we're here?" Reynolds asked.

"No," Maddox answered. "We're far enough out that they'd need long-range scanners to pick us out of the surrounding chaos."

"Any communications going back to the planet?"

"Nothing," Comm answered. "They're radio-silent."

Reynolds nodded and went back to watching the small mining ships at work. They spent several minutes on an asteroid before flitting off and landing on another, the process beginning afresh.

They looked like bees gathering pollen.

"There can't be much of whatever they're recovering out there," Jiya remarked, "or they'd stick around on a rock for more than minute or two, I'm thinking."

Takal agreed. "Trace amounts, it would appear. The holes they're leaving behind are shallow, not even a meter deep."

"Can we get a reading from here?" Reynolds leaned over Maddox's station, staring at the screen.

Maddox's fingers played across the console, and he shook his head a moment later. "There's too much interference from the asteroid field," he said. "Even locking onto the nearest of them was difficult, and the readings jump around too much to give me anything definitive."

"It's possible the mined material is throwing off the instrumentation," Takal explained. "I'd like to get a sample of it if possible."

Reynolds nodded his agreement. "I would too," he replied. "Ready a couple of bots to go out there and collect some once—"

"If I may?" Takal interrupted, raising a finger to get Reynolds' attention. "While the bots are the safest option available to us, I don't believe they are the best choice."

Reynolds stared at the inventor, one eyebrow raised, waiting for him to continue.

"The bots are limited in their storage capability," Takal went on. "If these people are willing to risk their lives," he gestured to the mining ships winding through the asteroid field, "to collect the substance, it stands to reason that it would behoove us to collect a substantial amount of it rather than just a small sample."

"We don't even know what the stuff is," Tactical complained. "It could be rock farts for all we know. We'd be putting our people at risk."

"All the more reason to obtain as much of it as we can in one go in order to fully examine it," Takal argued. "While the bots can collect enough for us to sample, if the substance has any use to us, we'll have to go back in person and collect more of it."

"It sounds like you expect the substance to be something that matters, and you'll want as much of it as you can get so you can play with it," Reynolds reasoned.

Takal shrugged. "Well, there *is* that. And the substance is matter, so we have that, too."

Reynolds chuckled. "Fine, ready a Pod and some bots and go get your mystery mineral. But," he pointed a finger at Takal for emphasis, "make sure it's not explosive or corrosive or any of the other '-ives' that would make me regret you bringing it aboard the ship."

"I'll be careful, I promise," the inventor assured the android, then spun on his heel and marched off to prepare the bots. "I'll be ready to go as soon as the alien ships have vacated the area."

Reynolds turned to Jiya. "Go with him and make sure he doesn't get into too much trouble."

"Yes, sir," she replied, hopping up and chasing after Geroux's uncle. "Wait for me."

She didn't think this was the right time to be doing this considering that Phraim-'Eh's cultists and the Loranian ship, the *Pillar*, could appear at any time, but she had to admit Takal's instincts were great when it came to sussing out materials that would benefit the crew and ship. They needed more pucks, and they needed to replace their missiles at a faster rate. They needed more and better raw materials.

As such, she decided to trust the nose of the old bloodhound when it came to finding what they were looking for. Besides, he needed someone to look after him.

Jiya and Takal waited until the mining ships had started back toward Muultar. No one knew how long they would be gone or if a second set of ships would take their place, so they knew they had to hurry.

Jiya piloted the Pod through the field of asteroids, her hands tightly clenched on the controls. She was glad the debris was fairly large, most of it bigger than the Pod. That made it easier to avoid than the radical smaller bits.

However, it meant screwing up had greater consequences.

One mistake, and an asteroid the size of a destroyer would get up close and personal to a most uncomfortable degree.

Rather than focus on that, she triggered her comm and reached out to Takal, who was a blur of motion in the back of the Pod while he prepared the bots.

"Everything okay back there?" she asked as she steered toward the asteroid that they'd determined was best suited for a safe Pod landing.

"The bots are ready to go," he replied, a tinge of excitement in his voice.

Jiya grinned. Although Takal wasn't the most adventurous of the crew, preferring to remain aboard the SD *Reynolds* and work on his inventions, there was nothing that thrilled him more than discovering something new he could tinker with.

"I have a containment device prepared, and I've added several additional scanners to the bots in order to determine if the substance is hazardous to us before we bring it aboard."

"Always a good thing," she fired back, chuckling.

Proximity warnings sounded as they neared their target, and Jiya silenced the alarm as she feathered her approach.

"We're coming up on the asteroid now," she transmitted to Reynolds. "Maybe it's a good idea to have Helm on standby in case I run into trouble landing this thing and securing our footing."

"You've got this," Reynolds encouraged her.

"How hard can it be, right?" She laughed. "Rhetorical question, Tactical!" she called right after. "I'm not looking for an answer."

Tactical sighed over the comm, but for once he kept his digital mouth shut.

Jiya eased the Pod toward the large asteroid, holding her breath. She hunkered down in her seat, one hundred percent of her focus on the space between.

The image of the gritty gray surface of the rock resolved as she closed and her scanner readings jumped wildly, giving her inconsistent and inaccurate information. Fortunately, she didn't need the scanner information to land, and none of the strange system's radiation affected the pilot's controls.

"Hold on tight, Takal," she called. "This could be bumpy."

The inventor muttered an affirmative and Jiya brought the Pod about, angling it to meet the momentum of the asteroid rather than attempting to chase the big rock down.

It came at them fast.

Jiya gulped and pulled back on the stick, bringing the

nose up at the last second and firing the thrusters to keep the asteroid from slamming into them.

The Pod reared back and matched the asteroid's speed an instant before the two collided, and Jiya looked stunned as she realized she'd timed the maneuver perfectly. She reduced the thrusters again as the ship continued to move, riding on the asteroid. She hadn't felt the landing.

The ship slid about a meter across the icy surface before the grapples deployed and speared the asteroid, bringing the Pod to a jarring halt.

Jiya exhaled hard as the stabilizers took hold and leveled the Pod.

"Well done," Takal murmured as he came from the back to stand alongside Jiya.

"I'm assuming you didn't die since I didn't see a flash," Tactical said over the comm.

"Nope," Jiya shot back. "Looks like we made it."

"No time to celebrate," Reynolds told her. "The mining ships have already reached Muultar. Get in and get out before they come back."

"Roger that," Jiya answered, turning to Takal. "Take your seat and get the bots moving. We're on the clock."

Takal nodded and went to work, manually operating the bots. He prepared to launch them from the Pod to excavate the surface of the asteroid. The goal was to find the substance the alien ships had been mining.

The bots exited the Pod and immediately began punching holes in the surface of the asteroid.

She felt a slush of jealousy for an instant as they drifted; she imagined they were the first beings to have ever landed on this particular asteroid.

It made her wish she'd brought along a flag to plant.

"I could be Queen of Rockville," she muttered under her breath.

"What's that?" Takal asked.

"Oh, nothing. Just talking to myself."

CHAPTER TWO

"Bring us around so we can cover the Pod better," Reynolds ordered. "I don't want those Muultarian ships sneaking up on them while they're stranded on that rock."

Ria brought up the thrusters, added power to the gravitic shields, and angled the *Reynolds* into the asteroid field.

He'd had his doubts about letting Takal and Jiya gather the mystery substance on their own, given the hostile environment and all the unknowns it presented, but he had to presume that Takal thought there was good reason for the jaunt or he wouldn't have suggested it.

He trusted the old man's judgment—most times—when it came to matters of science and invention.

The body he'd created for Reynolds was a marvel. Although it had yet to be tested in combat, it felt amazing.

It flowed with his thoughts like none of the previous incarnations had. It had become so much a part of him in the short time he'd been inside it that he had already begun to forget that it was there.

It felt natural, and seeing as how he was an AI and not a living being, that was saying something.

He wondered if this was how it felt to be human.

He clenched and unclenched his hands, grinning at the smoothness of the movement. The articulation was so seamless that he could only wonder what his new body was capable of.

Reynolds was anxious to find out, yet a nagging worry pecked at the back of his mind. What if he separated himself from the ship? Was it even possible?

Maybe he could give the maintenance functions away but keep his higher thought processes, passing those operational details to his alter egos. They had the brainpower and bandwidth to operate the ship.

Could he? If he could, should he?

For the first time since he'd been integrated into an android form, he found himself concerned for it.

The last thing he wanted to do was wreck the body.

He looked down at himself admiringly and sighed. With his decision to try it out, he had compartmentalized from the other aspects of his personality, as well as the ship, and began to think of himself as an individual.

It was strange.

Exciting and frightening at the same time, he had to admit.

He'd never be human, he knew that, but with the new body, he'd become so much more than an AI trapped in a mobile cage.

"How's it going out there?" Asya asked, interrupting Reynolds' introspection.

"So far so good," Jiya answered. "The bots have already

dug in, and they stumbled across something Takal can't identify. The scanners are still being affected, but nothing is coming back as dangerous so far."

"Good news," Asya replied. "Skies are clear. No alien ships inbound, at the moment anyway."

"I think I've determined why the Muultu are mining the substance," Takal cut in. "It appears to have inherent reflective capabilities."

"Going to need you to be more specific, Takal," Maddox told the inventor. "Right now, I'm picturing you using this stuff to keep people from bumping into shit in the dark."

Takal chuckled. "No, nothing like that. The ore seems to reflect small amounts of the system's radiation rather than absorb it. I'll need to examine it more closely to be certain, but it appears as if it can be used as radiation shielding to some degree."

"Which explains why the locals are willing to risk their lives to get it," Asya commented. "If all Muultu look like that melted-face guy, they can use all the shielding they can get."

"Imagine what they'd look like without it," Tactical pointed out, chuckling. "Eat your heart out, Pizza-the-Hutt."

Asya glanced over her shoulder at Tactical's position, despite knowing he wasn't actually there. "Were you dropped on your processor when you were little?" she asked. "I don't understand half the things you say."

"And you should ignore the other half." Maddox laughed.

"I think we need to add Earth Culture 101 to those lessons Jiya ordered for the crew," Tactical said.

"Why?" Asya countered. "So we know what you're talking about? No, thanks."

"How much longer until you have what you need, Takal?" Reynolds asked, cutting off the crew's chatter.

"Another fifteen minutes or so," the inventor answered. "The bots are finding it easy to collect the samples, given how close they are to the surface, but the density is low. They're having to range farther and farther from the Pod to collect enough to make it worth our efforts."

"Don't let them get too far away," Reynolds warned.

"It seems I can't even if I wanted to," Takal told the AI. "The radiation is distorting the command signals. I've had to suit up and step outside the Pod to keep the bots working. They're freezing up without a direct signal."

"You have an eye on him, Jiya?" Reynolds asked.

"I do," Jiya answered. "He's right outside, not more than two meters from the Pod's hatch. The bots are moving along smoothly now."

Reynolds nodded although he knew she couldn't see it. He glanced at Maddox. "Any sign of the mining ships?"

"Negative," the general answered. "I haven't picked up any activity near the planet since the others returned."

"Still no communications," Comm reported.

"Any clue what that ore is, Takal?" Reynolds asked.

"Not so far. It has a strange composition, oddly soft and pliable considering we're finding it under the frozen surface. It reminds me of gold in some ways, only more malleable. When we get back, I c...n tr...ir..."

Reynolds tapped the side of his head. "Comm, what's wrong with the comm?"

"There's nothing wrong with it," Comm replied. "Diagnostics show—"

"A big fucking rock!" Tactical shouted, bringing it up on the screen.

Reynolds stiffened. Out of nowhere, a massive asteroid cut between the superdreadnought and the smaller asteroid the Pod had landed on. The rock blocked both the comm signal between the two and the visuals.

"Get them out of there!" Reynolds ordered, knowing damn well there was nothing that could be done.

That didn't stop the crew from trying.

"Amplifying the signal, and I've launched a communications buoy to bounce our signal around that planetoid and reestablish the connection," Comm announced.

Reynolds growled. "Get a Pod out there in case…" He let the rest of his statement hang, knowing it wouldn't help morale to finish it.

He had to trust that Jiya and Takal would see what was going on and adjust accordingly.

"Pod launched," Maddox said. "Helm's at the controls."

"Can we blast this thing?" Reynolds questioned.

"Only if you want to squish the meatbags by sending hundreds of rocks streaking toward them instead of just one," Tactical answered.

"The asteroid is on a collision course with Jiya's Pod," Asya said.

"How the fuck did that thing sneak up on us? Tactical, get your head out of your ass," Reynolds snapped, baring his teeth.

"Working on it," Tactical fired back.

"Get us in front of that asteroid before it hits," Reynolds ordered.

"No time," Ria called back, even though the SD *Reynolds* had already begun to follow an intercept course.

"Damn it!" Reynolds growled.

Jiya and Takal were on their own.

Jiya had taken to watching Takal from the back of the Pod near the hatch.

The inventor had inched farther from the ship as he struggled to maintain the connection between the bots and the control box. He'd brushed off Jiya's warnings a number of times once he'd figured out how useful the ore he'd found might be.

Jiya chuckled at his dogged determination. He was so much like Geroux in that respect. Once either of them found something that interested them, they would go to the ends of the universe to satisfy their curiosity.

And as she'd often done with Geroux, Jiya gave the inventor some slack and let him wander, knowing she could use the bots to collect him quickly enough should anything happen.

She stood just inside the hatch as one of the bots dropped off its load of material into the containment box. A shadow fell over her as it did, and she shooed the bot off as it was blocking her vision.

It took her a moment to realize that the shadow didn't disappear after the bot's departure. In fact, it grew deeper.

She leaned out of the hatch and glanced up at the space

between the asteroids. Her heart sputtered when she realized there wasn't any.

All she could see was the gray stone of another asteroid streaking toward them.

"Takal!" she screamed, but it was too late.

The asteroid slammed into the one they were on with a resounding rumble that Jiya felt rather than heard.

She was thrown back into the Pod and crashed into the wall.

Stars swam before her eyes, and the breath was knocked from her lungs. The world spun around her, and her hands grasped futilely for something to stop her head-over-heels tumble.

She hit the roof before she found purchase, then the wall again, the floor, and the wall once more.

Every impact was as if she had been shot. Sharp pains tore through her and whited-out her vision. She heard a scream echoing in her ears and only realized a moment later that it was her own.

Then she fell into a corner and stayed there.

Everything around her spun for a moment longer as she was battered by the tools and equipment that had been lying loose in the back of the Pod. They clattered down around her, a metallic rain, and pieces of the ore the bot had been storing peppered her armor with tiny *plinks*.

Her head swam, and a loud ringing stabbed her ears. She struggled to get up, scattering the debris around her as she climbed to her feet.

Jiya clutched the wall beside her to stay upright. She regretted her insistence then and thought about flopping back to the floor. That was when she remembered the inventor.

"Takal!" she screamed over the comm despite the piercing agony it inflicted upon her brain. "Takal!"

She surged toward the hatch to look outside. Her stomach lurched at what she saw.

The Pod had broken free of its moorings and was floating out into space. She grabbed the frame of the door and swallowed hard.

The asteroid that had struck theirs had apparently only glanced it, but that had been more than enough to send her rock careening away.

Open space yawned beneath Jiya where semi-solid ground had been only moments before. She spotted a humanoid shape floating in the emptiness and recognized it as one of the bots.

"Oh…" she mumbled, knowing that Takal's fate had been the same as the bots.

She adjusted her optics and cast a frantic glance around. There were only seconds available to her before she lost Takal forever.

Then she spied him.

"Takal!" she screamed. "Make sure your transponder is on."

She marked his position as best she could, not getting a response, and dove back into the Pod. Her breath fogged the glass of her visor quicker than the system could clear it as she raced for the pilot's seat.

Jiya threw herself into it, not wasting any time engaging the restraints. She grabbed the controls, fired up the engines, made the most cursory of examinations as to her surroundings on the scanners, and shot off after the inventor.

"I'm coming, Takal," she called.

She didn't know if he could hear her, but she damn well wasn't going to leave him floating in space without a friendly voice to let him know rescue was on the way.

The comm crackled and Jiya's pulse roared, but it was Reynolds who came across the connection, not Takal.

"We're tracking him," the AI reported, updating the inventor's current position.

Jiya growled and adjusted her flight path. She'd been going off her estimated coordinates, and they hadn't been nearly close enough factoring in the drift of Takal's momentum.

"Biosystems show he's alive, but he doesn't appear to be conscious," Reynolds went on. "Heartbeat steady, oxygen at sufficient values. He hasn't sprung a leak."

That was the best news Jiya could hope for.

She thought for a second about having the bots go after him, but in the rush, she'd forgotten how limited their signals had been.

"That was what got us into this mess in the first place," she growled, furious at herself for letting Takal wander off. The bots were useless at this range with all the interfering radiation.

Jiya veered off sharply to avoid being struck by pieces of asteroid debris, then shifted back to follow Takal. The scanners told her there was another of the SD *Reynolds'* Pods a short distance behind her, but it wouldn't reach Takal any faster than she would, even with Helm piloting it.

"You have eyes on?" she asked.

"Negative," Reynolds came back. "His transponder's working, but the asteroid field is blocking our advance. Ria's afraid to barrel through for fear of stirring these rocks up even more."

As much as Jiya was grateful for the girl's thoughtfulness, to learn she wouldn't have the superdreadnought's muscle at her back sent a chill skittering up her spine. She hurt all over from getting thrown around, and she'd hoped to be relieved of having to do it all. Such was not to be her fate, however, so she clenched her jaw and willed the pain to a dull roar.

It was just her and Helm, and unless the AI's piloting personality had a bunch of bots aboard, he wouldn't be a whole lot of help—not that the bots would be either.

Jiya snarled as she hurried to where Takal was last reported. There was no way she was letting him go.

The asteroid field had other ideas, however.

As the Pod wound its way through the field, two nearby asteroids collided, banking one of them straight at the Pod.

Jiya nearly bit her tongue off as she veered sharply, only remembering at the last second that she wasn't strapped in.

She wrapped her legs around her chair and hung on for dear life as the Pod rolled. Her every muscle shrieked as her battered body struggled to remain seated.

The asteroid struck the rear of the Pod.

There was a loud metallic *crunch* as the upper back end of the Pod crumpled in on itself and sent the craft tumbling. Jiya gasped, amazed that she had managed to remain in position, although she wasn't sure her shoulders or legs appreciated the effort.

She fought the controls and brought it about, and a prayer slipped from her lips as she realized the engines were still functional. The asteroid had missed crushing them along with the top of the Pod.

"Location!" she screamed over the comm. "I need coordinates."

Silence answered her.

"Where's Takal?" she shouted again, her voice raw with emotion. She could taste copper in the back of her throat. "Where is he?"

"The transponder's gone silent," Reynolds told her.

The words were like hands of ice grasping her heart.

"No," she spat. "Find him!"

Jiya spun the ship and engaged the scanners, despite knowing they were effectively worthless in this patch of irradiated space.

She wasn't going to give up, though.

"Helm's going to continue the search," the AI told her. "You need to get that wrecked Pod back to the ship."

"I'm not leaving him out here," she argued.

"Neither are we," Reynolds shot back, "but we can't risk losing you—"

"Me too?" she interrupted, her cheeks flushing. "Was that what you were going to say?"

"Let Helm find him," Reynolds said, avoiding her question. "Return to the *Reynolds*. That's an order," he added.

Jiya ignored the commrand, although she stayed quiet to keep from outright defying the captain. She knew she needed to be professional and do what she was told. Reynolds meant well; he wasn't giving up on Takal, but Jiya couldn't help but see it that way.

If she turned around and left and Takal died…

No!

She wouldn't think that way. She refused to.

"He's out here, Reynolds," she told the AI. "He has to be. I'm going to—"

"Incoming!" Reynolds shouted across the link. "Pull back!"

Instinct kicked in and Jiya pulled back on the stick, reining in the Pod's forward momentum. She snarled and cursed and stomped her foot on the deck, furious that she'd been forced to halt her pursuit, but she'd had no choice, she realized, no matter how much she wanted to ignore that fact.

One of the alien mining ships appeared a short distance ahead of her, blocking her path.

She reached for the weapons controls, ready to blast the ship out of her way so she could continue her search, but a hollow thrumming buzz warned her of incoming communications. She opened the channel without thinking.

"You better have a damn good reason for impeding my passage," she snarled.

A deep, sonorous voice came back across the connection. "I assumed you wanted to know that your lost crewmember is safe aboard our vessel," the voice said. "Am I incorrect?"

"Takal?" Jiya gasped.

"Safe and sound, Jiya," the old inventor replied. "Safe and sound, thanks to my newfound friends here."

Jiya slumped in her seat with relief.

"Thank you," she muttered, barely able to get the words out. "Thank you."

CHAPTER THREE

"I am Gol Ato," the mining ship's pilot told Jiya. "And you are?"

"The name is Jiya Lemaire," she answered, "first officer of the SD *Reynolds*. That's the superdreadnought looming a short distance above us."

"What purpose do you have in Muultarian space?"

Jiya sighed. Just once she'd like to go someplace and not be challenged.

It wasn't like people showed up in orbit bearing gifts and good tidings very often.

"We're on a mission for our superiors," she replied, knowing she had to be careful what she revealed. Who knew what would set these aliens off? She couldn't afford to do that, especially seeing how they had Takal. "We're simply passing through your system and stumbled across the ore in the asteroids. We stopped to take a small sample, that's it."

"All of the devium in this system belongs to His Imperial Majesty Krol Gow," Gol announced. "It is a violation of his laws to collect or possess devium without royal consent."

Oh, hello there, foot in mouth. How I've missed you!

"We are not from your world...obviously, and did not know this," Jiya argued. "We would be glad to return the small amount we appropriated in exchange for our crewmember, and then we will gladly vacate your system."

She knew she shouldn't be speaking for Reynolds, seeing as how she couldn't picture the AI leaving the system until he learned more about Jora'nal, Phraim-'Eh, and the *Pillar*, the massive enemy ship that had been tailing them. But since these miners had Takal, there was no way she was going to defer the negotiation and delay his freedom.

"I'm afraid I cannot authorize such a trade," Gol told her. "The emperor's laws are absolute. He is the arbiter of all decisions, and I must abide by his will."

Of course, he is...

Jiya groaned. "I'll need to speak with my captain," she told the alien miner.

"So be it," Gol replied. "My crew is sending you coordinates now. Bring your chosen representatives in one of your Pods, within the hour, and do nothing to provoke the emperor's wrath or there will be dire consequences."

It's like every species works off the same handbook for how to handle alien encounters, Jiya thought.

"I'll return to my ship and inform my captain of your demands," she told the Muultu. "Make sure you keep my friend safe," she added with a snarl.

Gol said nothing in reply.

His ship turned about and shot back toward Muultar, weaving through the asteroid field with ease.

"Want me to follow them?" Helm asked.

Jiya did, but she knew it wasn't a good idea. "No," she replied. "We have our marching orders…for now."

Having thought she'd lost Takal, it infuriated her to have to leave him in the hands of some unknown alien race that had already proven they had people working for Phraim-'Eh who had participated in an effort to kill Reynolds and the crew.

But she knew the best thing she could do was return to the SD *Reynolds* and make a plan.

Together, they'd get Takal back.

"I'm already not liking these people," Geroux growled. She paced back and forth, her fists clenched, cheeks flaring with crimson dots. The bridge lighting was subdued and did nothing to dampen her internal fire.

"The fact that they rescued him bodes well," Reynolds said, assuming his role as the calming presence. "Had they wanted to hurt him, they could have left him out there."

"I feel better already," Jiya snarled.

Reynolds shrugged. "Well, it's the truth, shitty as it might sound." He held up his hand and locked eyes with Jiya. She unclenched her jaw, but her mouth continued to run away with her.

"I guess it's okay for them to hold him hostage in order to force our hand?"

"I didn't say it was," he shot back, cautioning her to rein

in her acerbic tongue. "I simply said that it's a good sign that they kept him alive, regardless of their reasoning. It gives us a chance to rescue him."

"By walking into who knows what," Asya countered. "This could be a trap."

"It could be," Reynolds replied, "but it wouldn't be the first one we've walked into, now would it?"

"I thought you were the one who wanted us to learn from our mistakes," Jiya argued.

"I do," he answered, "but sometimes we have to take a chance, especially when one of our crew is at risk. We don't leave anyone alive behind. *Ever!*"

Jiya was about to argue that that had been what Reynolds had suggested when he'd ordered her to pull back in the Pod, but she knew deep down that he hadn't. His order was to protect her life while recovery efforts were underway by remote control—the challenge of leadership that Reynolds, and Reynolds alone, had to carry. She grimaced at her lack of self-control.

When will I get my dumb ass under control? she thought and blew out a heavy breath, shaking her head at herself and not the captain.

Reynolds hadn't wanted to lose *two* of his crew and had made the difficult decision of risking that one of his people might die so that no others would.

Her stomach churned at the thought, but he had been right.

That was something she would have to learn one of these days: how to compartmentalize her feelings and make the hard calls to save lives, even if it meant losing someone close to her.

She hoped she would never have to make that call, but expected that one day she would.

"So, what do we do?" she asked, looking for options.

"We suit up and follow their directions," Reynolds answered matter of factly. "First, however, we bring the *Reynolds* closer to their orbit so we have the cavalry in position, and we scan the planet as best we can before we go down. Get the lay of the land."

Reynolds didn't wait for Jiya to agree. He gestured for Ria to follow his command, and the young ensign did just that.

"We go in guns blazing?" Ka'nak asked, slamming a fist into the palm of his hand.

"We prepare to blaze, but we go in like we always do," Reynolds corrected. "We try to trade first, and go from there."

"We're not putting my uncle in danger just so we can get into a fight," Geroux spat, glaring at the Melowi.

Ka'nak threw his hands in the air. "I wasn't implying we should," he told her. "I want the old guy back as badly as you do. He's my drinking buddy."

Geroux sighed, looked ready to berate Ka'nak again, especially about encouraging Takal's drinking, then simply went silent. She nodded to him.

"If we need to use force, we will," Reynolds assured everyone, "but let's exhaust our other options before that. No one needs to get hurt."

"Until they do," Tactical added.

"Until they do," Ka'nak parroted loudly.

"Until they do," Reynolds agreed, glancing at Geroux.

Jiya went over and gave her friend a fierce hug. "We'll get him back," she told her. "I promise."

Geroux sniffed and nodded, squeezing Jiya back.

"Muultar's a shithole," XO reported, his authoritative voice cutting through the sudden silence that had fallen over the bridge.

"Care to be a little more specific?" Reynolds asked.

"The radiation from the three suns has kicked the planet in its molten nuts," XO went on. "The atmosphere, while breathable by the crew, is like being hot-boxed by Cheech and Chong while Arnold Schwarzenegger lights up a long Cuban in the back seat."

"I'm not sure what language that was, so can you maybe say that again in one that the translators understand?" Jiya asked, glaring at XO's station.

"It's too harsh to breathe directly," Reynolds replied for XO. "Everyone keeps their helmets on at all times while exposed to the atmosphere."

"What about orbital defenses?" Asya asked.

"This place isn't designed to stand against an invasion," Tactical answered. "There are eight cruisers in orbit around the planet, but they might as well be rockets for all their effectiveness."

"What do you mean?" Jiya asked.

"The ships are junkers," Tactical said. "Old tech that was old tech when tech was old. We could go toe to toe with all eight ships at once and walk away without a scratch."

"Then why are we letting them hold Takal?" Ka'nak asked.

"Because they don't need a cruiser to kill *him*," Reynolds reminded. "We go down there and do what we have to do to collect him, then we're free to let Tactical loose on the Muultu if that's what we need to do. Until then, however, we're going to play nice. Understood?"

The crew grudgingly agreed to the captain's orders.

Reynolds grunted at their attitudes and turned back to Tactical. "Keep in mind that our primary mission, the reason we're here, is to find the Phraim-'Eh cult members and extract everything they know about the Kurtherians. I need that information, and I'll do what I have to in order to get it." Those on the bridge shifted uncomfortably, eyes darting around. "Tactical, what's the surface look like?"

"Like twice-roasted shit," Tactical replied. "The planet appears to be a giant floating volcano. There are pockets of civilization spread across Muultar that appear to be shielded to some degree, probably by the fancy element the professor found. Nothing as fancy as the Krokans, mind you, but some kind of atmospheric manipulation that keeps the worst of the heat and noxious fumes outside the barrier. The temperature and radiation levels are reduced at the population centers, although I'd still suggest staying covered."

"Is their tech level on the ground the same as in space?" Asya asked.

"Industrial-level tech all around, as far as I can tell. The planet barely gives off an energy signature, and while some of that might be due to the radiation levels, I'm not picking up anything that makes me think they've advanced beyond just getting into space."

"So, no Kurtherian energy signatures?" Reynolds asked.

"Nothing stands out," Tactical replied.

"Did the cultist lie to us?" Maddox asked aloud.

"Only one way to find out," Reynolds answered. "We go down to the planet and start asking questions."

"About damn time!" Geroux growled.

"Standard landing team, get your gear and head to the Pods," Reynolds ordered. "We'll finalize our plans there."

Geroux stomped off, and Jiya followed her. She wanted to get Takal back as badly as her friend did, and she swore they'd stop at nothing to accomplish that.

No one kidnaps my crew!

The Pod dropped toward the surface of Muultar, giving the crew a good close-up of the planet.

Jiya didn't like what she saw.

"This place is damn ugly," she muttered, aghast at the geological hostility.

The sky shone a dusky red as the Pod carrying Jiya, Maddox, Reynolds, and L'Eliana broke through the atmosphere. Jiya could feel the engines straining against the pollutants in the air. It made the craft sluggish, and she fought the controls more than she'd anticipated.

"It's like flying through mud," she commented. "I hope the engines hold up."

"They will," Reynolds assured her, but the look on his face was less than promising.

Jiya followed the coordinates they had been provided and steered the Pod toward the edge of the nearest city. It was hard to see, even with the ship throwing up a 3-D view of their surroundings. There was simply too much ash and dust in the air.

"I'm not detecting much in the way of city defenses," Jiya reported.

"The tech's too low to pinpoint it," Reynolds clarified. He tapped the viewscreen, pointing out several small areas on the image of the city. "Those look like anti-aircraft outposts."

"Firing what?" Jiya asked. "Missiles?"

"Looks that way. Maybe even chemical-explosion-driven hard projectiles."

"Wow." Jiya shook her head in disbelief. "Do they actually expect to hit anyone with those?"

"In this sludge?" Maddox replied. "Quite possibly."

"I'm not sure I can fly in this," L'Eliana admitted, staring wide-eyed out the window.

"You shouldn't have to," Jiya reassured her. "The atmosphere inside the city barrier isn't as soupy. If we're going to need you to fly the ship, it'll be there."

L'Eliana forced a smile. Her lack of certainty was obvious, and Jiya felt bad for her.

It didn't matter how much training a person had; until they built up their confidence, every task seemed daunting.

It had been that way for Jiya early on, but she was determined to succeed and prove her father wrong about everything.

L'Eliana needed a little extra motivation, and experience was the only way to get it.

Jiya smiled her way. "You'll do fine, don't worry."

The Pod trudged through the sky, finally breaking through the hazy barrier that surrounded the capital city of Ulf.

Jiya gasped when the controls immediately loosened

and she almost lost control of the Pod, having not realized just how hard she'd been fighting the stick. The ship veered hard to starboard, nearly throwing it into a spin.

"Easy there," Reynolds called as Jiya regained her composure and brought the Pod about, correcting its drift.

"I meant to do that," she muttered, wiping the sweat from her forehead.

"Well, don't mean to do that ever again," Reynolds told her. "I just got this body, and I'd like to get some use out of it before you take it for a dip in some molten lava pit."

"Gotcha." She gave him a thumbs-up. "We're coming in for a landing."

Although the air had cleared considerably, the atmospheric wall between the outside world and Ulf holding back the majority of the bad air, there was still a reddish-gray pall within the barrier.

"Scanners show the air is decent enough to take off our helmets in here, but it won't be pleasant," Jiya reported.

"Let's leave that until we're inside the buildings, then," Reynolds ordered. "I don't need us rescuing Takal just to have the rest of you spending time in the Pod-doc repairing your lungs."

"Can't say I'm interested in that," Maddox muttered. "Helmets on, it is."

"You stay suited up, too," Jiya told L'Eliana, "even with the Pod sealed. Just to be safe."

L'Eliana nodded. "Safe is good."

Jiya couldn't agree more.

She brought the Pod in for a landing and settled easily onto the directed parking apron at the spaceport. After the effort of setting down on the asteroid, landing on a broad, stable surface was a treat.

Once they were on the ground, she cycled the engines and relinquished her seat to L'Eliana, who plopped down with a nervous giggle. Jiya grabbed her shoulder and gave a gentle squeeze.

"It'll be all right," she told her.

"Our hosts are waiting outside," Reynolds informed.

Jiya went through the ritual of checking her weapons and equipment, making sure she was ready for anything before they exited the Pod.

She glanced at Maddox, who nodded his readiness, and Reynolds forced a grin.

"Guess it's time to make nice," the AI said. "Go ahead and open the hatch, L'Eliana, and then seal it behind us."

"Yes, sir," she replied. "Good luck."

The crew exited the Pod quickly, not giving any of their hosts the opportunity to get a look inside before the hatch was shut and locked.

Jiya was surprised to find they hadn't even tried.

A handful of people stood casually on the tarmac waiting for the crew. And like those they had seen on Krokus 1, all of the Muultu looked as if their faces had been attacked by blowtorches.

Their skin was red and raw and seemed to run with open wounds, the cracks and crevices gleaming with moisture. Yellow eyes stared out of stoic faces, and despite the calm nature of the Muultu, there was a natural appearance of fury that emanated from them. They looked hostile despite doing nothing to back up that perception.

Resting scorch face, Jiya thought, fighting her inner being to remain calm.

The ship that had brought the Muultu back to the planet with Takal sat a short distance away, but there was no sign of the inventor.

"He is well taken care of, fear not," a Muultu said as if reading her mind. Jiya recognized his smooth voice as that of Gol Ato. Its softness belied the impression his face expressed.

Jiya nodded and motioned to the crew with her. "This is General Maddox," she introduced, then gestured to Reynolds. "This is the captain of the SD *Reynolds*, Reynolds."

Gol smiled, Jiya assumed, although the effect was a hideous mockery of kindness. It sent a shudder through Jiya's body. "Your ship is named after you? You must be a great warrior."

"The greatest, but my humility keeps me from admitting it," Reynolds fired back, not bothering to hide his grin.

Gol chuckled. "I see that, but I must warn you, the emperor will not find such attempts at humor amusing. I would be careful."

"I'm guessing no emperor does," Maddox commented. "It must be part of the package: become emperor, check your sense of humor at the door."

"Not all emperors are humorless," Reynolds corrected. "Though, technically, the one I'm thinking of calls herself a Queen now, so maybe there is something to that theory."

"We'll have to meet her one day," Jiya said.

Reynolds nodded pleasantly. "You will."

Gol and his compatriots closed on the crew. "We must insist upon collecting your weapons."

"Of course," Reynolds replied, stripping off his belt and handing it over, his pistol still holstered.

Jiya hated this part of treating with new races. She never felt good about disarming the moment they entered a strange ruler's domain, but she understood it.

She slipped the rifle off her back and did the same as Reynolds, handing over her whole belt, gun included.

Fortunately, Takal had built numerous secret compartments into the suits of armor he'd adapted and, while no one could see or detect them, Jiya was comforted by the fact that she was never truly without a weapon as long as she remained snug inside her personal suit of high-tech armor.

Once Gol and his people had collected the weapons, they marched the crew across the tarmac toward an enclosed vehicle.

Jiya couldn't help but stare as they approached it.

She'd never seen anything so...archaic.

A great pillar rose from the front of the heavy steel vehicle, the stack blowing out thick gray smoke. The engines rumbled loudly enough to vibrate the ground, and the chassis barely budged when they were led up a short flight of steps into the back.

A cockpit of sorts was positioned ahead of the large cabin where the crew sat, and two Muultu crowded into the front as the crew took a seat. There was a loud grinding of gears, and the vehicle lurched forward through a billow of its own smoke. Metal treads ground across the tarmac.

No one said a word as they traveled, the vehicle being far too loud for conversation.

Of all the strange things Jiya had seen since joining Reynolds on his quest to find Kurtherians, this was by far the strangest.

A race that lives on the surface of an active volcano being torn apart by the gravity from three suns. While supposedly spacefaring, they can barely travel from one point to another in technology from the era of steel. Where the hell are we?

CHAPTER FOUR

Jiya had been surprised by the lack of guards or soldiers around the landing port, but she soon realized that was because there weren't any ships worth stealing.

When they left the tarmac, the strange vehicle passed through a heavily-guarded checkpoint where dozens of soldiers stood at attention. They were dressed in suits of armor that reminded her of the vehicle they were riding in: cold, heavy, and far too clunky to be effective.

The raw numbers, however, made it look impressive.

Jiya stared out the back of the open vehicle, watching the checkpoint disappear into the distance as they trundled farther into the city.

The whole of Ulf was built as if it were intended to stand against an orbital bombardment or nuclear attack.

Perhaps it was.

Seeing as how the entire planet was a massive volcano, lava flowing freely outside the barrier, Jiya could imagine the whole place being swallowed by molten rock. It made sense to build it to industrial standards.

Steel and brick were used with abandon, with little to no wood appearing in the construction of the buildings they passed. What little organic matter was used was for decoration rather than stability.

There was little of that, either.

The city was utilitarian in design. All the buildings looked the same, and Jiya often couldn't tell what was a business and what was someone's home.

People stared at them as they rolled by, maybe since theirs was the only vehicle on the road. The citizens stood on the narrow walks alongside soldiers, who mixed freely with the people.

No one looked happy, but given the nature of their scorched faces, she wasn't sure if that was because they weren't or if they all just looked that way.

Could be either.

She did notice a number of people in the crowd who weren't Muultu, the lack of charred faces being the give-away, but they didn't look much better off. Their skin was browned from the heat, and they wore long, flowing robes to cover the entirety of their bodies.

They didn't look much happier to see the crew than the native Muultu.

Jiya looked away after a short time, realizing she wasn't likely to see a smiling face.

The ride through town seemed to take forever, especially given how loud the vehicle was. They rode without talking, everyone staring at the city as if trying to map their way back to the landing field.

While everything looked exactly the same, Ulf was built on a perfectly uniform grid. All one needed to do was get pointed in the right direction and follow the road to its end.

There was no way to get lost.

After a while, Jiya's eyes glazed over at the sameness of everything and she slumped on her bench, waiting for the ride to be over. When it finally was, she clambered out of the vehicle, ready to leave the planet Muultar behind.

She'd seen more than enough.

"This way," Gol yelled as the vehicle pulled away. He ushered the crew through yet another checkpoint and into a large courtyard that sprawled beyond.

Marble statuary ran along the edges, all cut from a dark stone. Like everywhere else they'd seen, there was no hint of vegetation anywhere.

"I wonder how they eat?" Maddox whispered.

Jiya shrugged, not having an answer to the question and hoping they wouldn't be there long enough to care.

Gol and the others led the crew into the courtyard and through a large arched entryway that led inside. The hazy red of the light shifted only slightly, taking on a yellowish pall as lighted sconces illuminated the way.

Jiya goggled at the idea that people still used actual fire to light their homes. She was glad her tinted visor blocked her face from view.

"This place is absolutely medieval," Reynolds whispered over the comm.

Their footsteps thumped on the stone floors as Gol ushered them through a long hallway and up to a pair of massive steel doors that towered over the crew.

Jiya marveled at the craftsmanship and ran her eyes along the frame, admiring the symbols that were raised from the door. A menagerie of animals, many of which Jiya couldn't recognize, was the focus, and the magnificent designs almost made her stumble into Maddox's back when the crew stopped.

Two of the males with Gol pushed, grunting, and the massive portal swung open about half a meter before the pair stopped pushing. Some mechanical device took over from there.

There was a hiss and a thump, then the doors inched open with a stuttering consistency that made Jiya think they were on tracks of some kind.

Her guess was proven correct when Gol waved them inside, revealing a pair of shallow metal grooves in the floor on which the massive portals moved.

The doors *thumped* into the wall, echoing loudly, and the crew were marched into a great hall that loomed even higher than the hallway outside.

Like everything else in Ulf, steel and dark stone dominated the construction materials.

Jiya wondered how long it had taken to build such a monstrous chamber without the assistance of bots or modern machines. She could only imagine, grateful she hadn't been one of the people made to work on it.

An aisle of red carpet ran down the center of the chamber, leading to a raised dais where seven large hewn-stone chairs were arrayed in a semi-circle. Two males and five females occupied the seats, the oldest of them situated in the central seat. All were Muultu, their waxen faces looking down on the crew. Was it disdain? No one could tell, given the perpetual terrifying scowl of the Muultu visage.

Armored guards ringed the walls, cold eyes staring as the crew advanced. Jiya glanced around, luxuriating in the privacy her helmet provided her for the moment. She was sure she would have to take it off once they were face to face with the emperor and whoever the rest of the seated people were, but until then, she was going to take advantage.

With no tapestries or flags or banners hiding the walls, all the exits were obvious in the sparseness of the décor. There were two large doorways, half the size of the main entry, to each side of the room, where the majority of the guards stood poised. Then there were two more to the back of the chamber, behind the chairs.

That didn't leave the crew many options if things went south.

Gol raised a hand for Reynolds and his people to halt at the foot of the dais' steps, and he turned and bowed to the people in their seats.

"Your Imperial Highness and honored Council, I bring you the trespassers we caught in the devium fields."

Jiya sighed at the introduction. Successful negotiations didn't often start with being called trespassers.

Reynolds removed his helmet, and Maddox and Jiya did the same.

They were off to a great start.

The oldest of the males rose from his seat and stared out at the crew. He got straight to the point. "What is your purpose here, strangers?"

Reynolds offered a shallow nod of respect. "I am Reynolds, captain of the Superdreadnought *Reynolds*, an Etheric Federation ship tasked with a mission by my

Queen, Bethany Anne. These are my crew, First Officer Jiya Lemaire and General Maddox," he announced, gesturing to each in turn. "We did not mean to intrude upon your resource field, and apologize for our ignorance and any disrespect we might have unintentionally shown. We only sought to examine the substance you call devium, nothing more."

You can sure pour it on when you want, can't you, Reynolds? Jiya chuckled to herself.

The emperor stared for a moment, his yellow eyes glaring in the flickering firelight, before he finally relented and returned Reynolds' nod.

"Your crew member Takal told us as much," Emperor Krol Gow replied. "He insisted the decision had been his and claimed full responsibility for it."

"While that might be true, Takal works for me," Reynolds countered. "He was there at my behest."

"Fair enough, Reynolds, but I did not mean that as a threat to your man," the emperor went on. "I am appreciative of both his honesty and your integrity." He waved them up the stairs. "Please, come and join us so we can stop yelling up and down the steps."

Jiya fought back her grin at her earlier thought that everyone they'd come upon had been hostile to them. The emperor's friendly offer caught her off-guard.

The crew tromped up the stairs to stand before the emperor, keeping a respectful distance from him. The other members of the council rose and came over, gathering around Krol Gow.

"I am Emperor Krol Gow," the oldest male said. He motioned to the people around him, starting with the older female who stood nearest. "This is Aht Gow, my sister and the speaker of my advisory council. Beside her are Chae Dun and Qui Na," he said, introducing the two males on the council. "The remainder of my council are Blu Ta, Fra Sa, and El Hi," he stated, pointed to each of the females in turn.

The blur of names was difficult for Jiya to keep up with, made worse by the fact that all of the Muultu looked quite similar due to the degenerative effects of the atmosphere. There was little to tell any of the council apart save for the clothing they wore, and even that was similar, down to the shiny red sashes they displayed, which started at their shoulders and draped across their chests to their waists.

Fortunately, each of the council had an identifying crest embroidered on their sleeves, which Jiya assumed were family crests since both of the Gows displayed the same one.

"Forgive my bluntness, Emperor," Reynolds said, "but I'd like to know that Takal is well before we go any further."

The emperor chuckled, looking almost jovial for a moment. "Of course."

He motioned to a guard standing out of sight behind the row of chairs, and the soldier went to one of the doors at the back of the room. He pulled the door open and waved. A moment later, Takal appeared, grinning. He and the guard made their way over, the soldier stepping away to let Takal walk the last few meters alone.

"I knew you'd find your way to me soon enough." He laughed as he joined the crew.

Jiya embraced him, taking a moment to examine the old

inventor before letting him go. "Geroux will kill me if I don't make sure you're okay," she told him.

"I'm fine," Takal told her, patting her hand reassuringly. He turned to the emperor and the others. "His Imperial Majesty has been nothing but a gentleman since I've been here."

"Good to hear," Reynolds said, returning his attention to the emperor. "Thank you for that."

The emperor nodded again, but his pleasant expression had faded. "You are most welcome, but I have to ask what brings you to our system? It is not often that we have visitors passing through."

Jiya glanced at Reynolds, wondering what he'd tell the emperor.

They had come to the planet chasing information on Jora'nal and the would-be god, Phraim-'Eh, but she didn't think that'd be the best thing to open with.

"We have a couple of purposes for being in your system," Reynolds replied, playing the role of politician, every word smooth. "The first of which is to open trade between us and the populated worlds within this galaxy to create a safe haven for our ship so we can restock and make any necessary repairs as we go about our mission."

"And your other purpose?" the emperor pressed.

Reynolds paused for a moment.

"We've come following a lead to a cult that has engaged us multiple times, putting my ship and crew in harm's way. We seek information on their whereabouts."

Jiya was shocked to hear him speak the truth so plainly.

"A cult?" Krol Gow asked, eyes narrowed. "What is the name of this cult you seek?"

"They call themselves the Cult of Phraim-'Eh," Reynolds replied.

The emperor shrugged at the name, as did the majority of the council behind him, but Jiya saw one of the females stiffen, eyes widening for an instant before she got her expression under control.

It was Aht Gow, the emperor's sister.

Jiya cast furtive glances her way to keep from staring outright, but Aht mastered her surprise so quickly that Jiya wondered if she had imagined it.

"I know of no such cult on our world," Emperor Krol Gow stated. "We are an isolated system with little to offer travelers in the way of resources or tourism, hence our need to protect what we have so fiercely. There is no reason for such a cult to come here."

Except for that isolated part, Jiya thought. That alone made Muultar the perfect location to recruit disciples. *Who* wouldn't *want to leave this burning rubbish pile of a planet?*

"We don't believe the cult has been established here," Reynolds went on. "However, we think it might well be a recruiting ground. We're certainly not accusing your government of anything."

Krol Gow nodded his understanding. "I didn't think you were, but I don't believe it would be possible for such wayward efforts to germinate here. Our people are focused on survival and making the most of what we've been given. To spend time and energy on the frivolous pursuit of a foreign religion seems...absurd when there are so many other concerns to occupy the people's time."

"I understand," Reynolds conceded, "but so you know, we recently stumbled across a number of your people who were involved in the cult. They operated against us openly in the Krokus system, so it's best you be aware."

"I will look into it personally, I can assure you," the emperor promised. "If we are to be unwittingly dragged into a war between these cultists and your Federation, I want to know all I can about such possibilities."

"The Federation has no designs to war on peaceful nations," Reynolds assured the emperor. "We're not here to start a fight, only to track down those responsible for recent attacks upon us."

"That's good to know," Krol Gow replied. "As for us, we have no interest in being used as anyone's pawns, nor forced to fight a battle that holds no advantage for us."

Reynolds acceded to the obvious truce, but it was clear he wasn't done yet.

"Have you heard of a being named Jora'nal?" the AI questioned. "He is an alien who masqueraded as a Loranian."

Once again, Jiya saw Aht Gow twitch, and this time, she was sure of it.

She knows something.

Jiya shifted slightly to get a clearer view of the emperor's sister, but once more she had reined in her surprise and presented the stoic pose of the rest of the advisory council.

"I have not heard the name," the emperor answered, shaking his head. "I will add it to my inquiry. As for the other reasons for your arrival, those are topics I can discuss with some certainty." The emperor smiled.

Reynolds returned the smile.

"As I said before, we have little to offer that might

interest a race of beings as advanced as you, but with some conversation, we may be able to find things that might be mutually beneficial." Krol Gow took a step forward. "What do you have to offer in return?"

Jiya could tell Reynolds liked the guy. He went straight to the point.

"We have a level of technology that can make the lives of you and your people better here on Muultar. We also have people who might be able to modify your atmospheric shield to make things more comfortable here."

Jiya stifled a grin when Reynolds didn't announce that it was Takal he was talking about. No point in dangling the inventor in front of them, seeing as how they had just released him.

Reynolds laid out a few of the advances he had to trade, avoiding, as usual, any mention of the more sophisticated technologies such as the Pod-docs, the Gate drives, or the nanocytes. The latter Jiya only knew by name and reputation.

"I would need to confer with my council before I make any final decisions, of course," the emperor said.

"Of course," Reynolds replied.

Krol Gow gestured to the guard who had retrieved Takal. "Find our guests comfortable accommodations and have the servants see to their needs," he commanded before turning back to the crew. "Please, follow the guard to your quarters and make yourselves at home. I will reach out to you as soon as I have had time to speak with my people."

"Thank you," the AI answered. "We look forward to treating with you."

The emperor nodded and moved off with his advisors

while the crew was ushered back through the massive doors and down the hall.

Jiya kept a careful eye on the emperor's sister until she was out of sight, and she caught the female staring back before the doors were closed.

The emperor might not know what was going on, but Jiya had no doubt they were in the right place.

CHAPTER FIVE

"This is some serious déjà vu," Maddox muttered as the crew were led into a host of suites to the side of the royal compound.

"Only in a rather austere way," Takal added, glancing around the stone and steel room. "Our hosts have quite the stout sensibility."

Reynolds raised a hand, calling for the crew's silence. He traipsed around the edges of the joined rooms, examining everything as he made his circuit. A few minutes later, he came back and gave them the okay.

"Did you really think they'd have listening devices or cameras in such a backwater place like this?" Jiya asked.

Reynolds shook his head. "No, but I *did* expect there to be viewing ports or secret passages that would allow the emperor's people to listen in and observe us." He shrugged. "I'm a bit surprised not to find any, to be honest."

"So, you think Gol Ato was bluffing when he implied the emperor was foul-tempered and cruel?" Maddox asked.

"I believe he is a bit in awe of us," Reynolds admitted. "It's clear the Muultu are not technologically advanced, and I think the emperor is smarter than to bluff when we know their capabilities. He's not looking to make enemies of people who can destroy him without much effort. A direct confrontation with us doesn't benefit him."

"Did you see how his sister reacted to the talk about the cultists?" Jiya wondered.

Reynolds nodded. "I saw her flinch, both when the cult was mentioned and when Jora'nal's name was brought up. She knows something."

"I wonder if the emperor does, too?" Jiya mused.

"He doesn't appear to, but then again, he might just be an accomplished liar," Reynolds went on. "I don't believe so, though."

"He seemed quite forthright to me," Takal stated, "although we didn't discuss politics or anything beyond our general purpose here in the system and answering a few questions regarding our technical capabilities, which I limited to generalities," he assured the AI. "I spent more time with the guard Pal We than I did the emperor or his council, admittedly."

"And you didn't hear anything from him, did you?" Reynolds asked.

Takal shook his head. "Only that we were waiting for you to arrive. They treated me kindly but left me in the dark. I only knew you'd shown up when Pal We came to fetch me."

Reynolds grunted. So far, they had little to work with. That frustrated him.

The cultist had led them to Muultar for a reason. He wondered if maybe they were being led into a trap, or if the cultist they'd captured had told them about Phraim-'Eh and Jora'nal as a distraction, something for them to waste their time on instead of tracking down the truth.

He didn't think that was the case, either.

The cultist was a fanatic, obviously. Reynolds didn't believe him capable of anything but blind devotion to his god and leaders. After all, he had killed himself to avoid revealing more than he already had in his frothing rant.

He didn't strike Reynolds as being capable of subtlety.

When the room had quieted, Maddox went over and flopped into a seat and groaned. "At least this is better than that last place we were holed up in," he announced, grinning as he leaned back in the chair. "Minus the food and the whole rebellion part."

"Speaking of your feeling of déjà vu," Reynolds said, "I think it time to reach out to the rest of the crew and see how things are going."

Jiya nodded and activated her comm. "Hey, Geroux. Did your team make it down to Muultar okay?"

The young tech came back a moment later. "No problems at all. You were right; the planet doesn't have any tech remotely advanced enough to detect a cloaked Pod, especially not in that maelstrom out there that they call their atmosphere. We didn't even catch a hint of scanners pinging us."

"Where are you now?" Reynolds asked.

"The Pod is parked in a vacant corner of the landing field, not far from where yours is. San Roche is on standby in it, and he reports that no one has approached L'Eliana since you left.

"We followed you to the royal palace, or whatever they call that monstrosity of rock and metal you're in. I'm kind of surprised that the comms work as well as they do, given all the natural interference of the building. It's probably that atmospheric barrier clearing up the signal."

"No need to analyze it. Just be grateful they do," Maddox commented.

Reynolds grinned at a plan well concocted and enacted.

Jiya had suggested the remainder of the crew—Asya, Geroux, Ka'nak, and San Roche—follow them down in the cloaked Pod, much as they had done on Krokus-1 recently. Given the lower level of tech displayed by the Muultu, she determined they could meet with the emperor and see how things went while having a small crew back them up, just in case.

With no idea what they were walking into, it had seemed the smart play.

"We had a bit of trouble keeping up with you through town, with so many people and soldiers out and about. This place is crowded for being such a toasty hellhole. Fortunately, the streets are barren. I didn't see a single vehicle the whole way except the one that carted you in."

"See anything weird on your way through Ulf?" Maddox asked.

"Besides people who look like they've spent too much time up close and personal with a leaky nuke?"

"Yes, besides that." Maddox chuckled.

"If you're asking if we saw any obvious cult activity, then no, we didn't," Geroux answered. "The Muultu seem to be relaxed with regards to their condition, but citizens who were obviously not born here all dress more or less the same, wearing loose, draping outfits that cover all but their faces. There's no uniformity to the clothing other than trying to ward off the heat and radiation."

"The place seems pretty open if a bit subdued," Asya added. "What conversations we overheard as we walked cloaked through the city were mundane, people talking about work, politics, and the daily grind. Damn boring, if you ask me."

"So, no one mentioned any secret plans or cult meetings, mass sacrifices, or planetary coups?" Jiya joked.

"I wish," Asya replied. "That would make this far more interesting, not to mention easier."

"I also didn't see any propaganda or graffiti or anything posted around the place," Geroux went on. "Either the rulers have an iron fist, or folks are content with their lives here and are willing to toe the imperial line."

Jiya shrugged at the comment, but Reynolds didn't know what was the case either.

So far, he'd had little indication that Emperor Krol Gow was a tyrant, but there *were* some signs of authoritarian rule. Still, that wasn't any of Reynolds' business. He wasn't in this galaxy to redefine planetary politics. He was in search of Kurtherians.

Regardless, while he and the rest of the crew dealt with the emperor, he needed the others to be his eyes and ears on the outside.

"One of the emperor's advisors—his sister actually— acted strangely when we brought up Phraim-'Eh and his cult and that rusty prick, Jora'nal," Reynolds said. "I'd like you to stake out the building and see if she leaves."

"She's wearing a long sandy-brown dress that does nothing to offset her melted face," Jiya added with an amused grin.

"That's helpful," Asya commented.

"She's wearing a red sash over her shoulder, and she has a crest patch on her arm. It looks like a bird with flaming wings surrounded by a black circle."

"A phoenix," Reynolds clarified.

"So, a bird with wings that are on fire?" Asya shot back. "Gotcha."

"You people are making me agree with Tactical, and I don't appreciate it," Reynolds grunted. "Mandatory Earth studies are next on the list of things to do."

"Boo," Maddox joked. "If Earth were so damn important, it'd be the center of the universe."

"Does it help that many people living there believe it is?" Reynolds fired back, grinning.

"Not really, no," Maddox answered, leaning back in his seat.

Reynolds conceded for the moment. "Keep an eye out for the sister, Asya, and let us know if you see anything you think we need to know about. I don't know how long we'll be here while the emperor and his people discuss our offers, so we don't want to miss anything important."

"Outside of a bunch of guard traffic, you're not missing anything," Asya reported with a bored sigh. "There's nothing exciting going on around here."

"That just means our enemy is doing a good job of hiding their efforts on Muultar," Reynolds countered. "Stay vigilant, and remain in contact. We don't want to lose comms."

"Roger that," Asya replied, closing the connection.

"So, what do we do now?" Jiya asked.

"We wait," Reynolds replied.

"And nap," Maddox added, letting his head loll on the back of the couch. He was unconscious a moment later.

"It must be nice to be able to sleep anywhere." Jiya moaned, watching the general, still amazed that he had crashed so easily.

"It's a soldier thing," Reynolds told her with a shrug. "When there's an opportunity for soldiers to squeeze in a nap, they do."

"I'm so jealous," Jiya complained, listening to her crewmate snore.

She'd never been able to simply pass out on command, but she wished she could. Of course, with all the damn snoring, she didn't figure she would have slept well anyway.

"You trust this Krol Gow?" she asked Reynolds, looking for a distraction.

He shook his head. "No more than I do any of the leaders we come across," he admitted. "In this case, though, because there are no obvious Kurtherian energy signatures emanating from the planet, I believe he might well be in the dark as to what's going on."

"Even with his sister being involved?"

"We don't know that she is yet," Reynolds answered. "She most definitely acted suspicious, but that doesn't mean Jora'nal or Phraim-'Eh have any real connection to the planet. She could have heard of them from another source, or maybe she travels. There are a number of reasons she could have acted the way she did."

"You believe that?" Jiya asked.

The AI chuckled. "No, not really," he admitted. "She was subtle about masking her reactions, but they were still too extreme to be ignored. She knows something, but I'm not sure yet how we can go about finding out."

"Foot in the ass?" Jiya suggested.

Reynolds grinned. "If it comes to that, but I think we're going to have to try a more subtle approach. The last thing we need is to offend the emperor. We can't go pointing fingers at his sister without any kind of evidence unless we want to stir shit up."

"And if he's not involved…" Jiya said, letting her thought fade.

"Exactly," Reynolds replied. "Why rattle his cage if we don't have to? All we'll do is screw up our chance at negotiations and, more importantly, make another enemy. We don't need more enemies in this galaxy."

Takal sighed. "I wish I'd spent more time with him."

"You said he asked you about our tech?" Jiya asked, remembering what Takal had said earlier.

The inventor nodded. "He had never seen a super-dreadnought before, apparently," Takal answered. "He was ignorant of its power, so I explained it in the simplest terms—mainly to ensure he understood what would happen should he decide to harm me." Takal laughed.

Jiya chuckled. "I guess that explains why he's being so nice. He doesn't want to have his kingdom blown out from under him."

There was a quiet knock on the door before Reynolds

had the opportunity to reply, and Takal went over and eased it open. Reynolds was surprised to see the emperor standing there with a half-dozen soldiers at his side.

This can go one of two ways, Reynolds thought. *He's come to kill us, or he needs something.*

Krol Gow slipped inside the room with his soldiers, one of them closing the door behind him. The emperor looked flustered and nervous.

The latter it is, Reynolds thought gladly.

As much as he wanted to find more of the cultists and wreak havoc on them while learning more about Phraim-'Eh, Reynolds wasn't spoiling for a fight with the Muultu if he could avoid it.

"What can we do for you, Emperor?" Reynolds asked.

Maddox stirred and came over to stand behind Reynolds and alongside Jiya and Takal.

"I ask that you come with me," he responded. "There is something I wish to discuss with you where no eyes can see or ears hear."

Interesting.

Reynolds nodded his agreement, and the emperor seemed relieved. One of his guards propped open the door and glanced outside. He waved them on a moment later, and the whole of the crew, the emperor, and the soldiers left the guest chambers and started down the corridor the opposite direction from which they had come.

Krol Gow led them to a blank wall, and he laid his hand upon it. There was a muffled *click* and the wall swung open, revealing a darkened tunnel beyond. The emperor didn't hesitate. He slipped through the secret passage and starting down the black hallway.

Although there were no lights save one in the distance, Reynolds could see the emperor and the corridor clearly. Once he was certain there was no one lying in wait for them, he and the crew followed, and the guards shut the secret door, staying close to the crew.

Reynolds felt the calmness of his convictions.

He'd been right to be patient.

CHAPTER SIX

"We're on watch duty for the foreseeable future," Asya announced to Geroux, who only nodded, having heard the order over the comm.

"Yay!" she joked, pulling a face.

The pair, along with Ka'nak, had staked out the top of a nearby building that had a good view of the one the rest of the crew had entered.

While Geroux didn't have a perfect line of sight to what might be happening on the other side of the compound, she could see the only other exit. Her advanced optics zeroed in; she would know if the emperor's sister or anyone else left the compound and traveled into the city.

While they waited, she split her focus on her surroundings, watching the people of Ulf go about their daily tasks, the soldiers making their rounds within the compound.

It wasn't any more exciting than what the rest of the crew were up to, but this was Geroux's least favorite aspect of the missions they went on.

"I wonder if the emperor is feeding them," Ka'nak said

wistfully, staring at the sky from where he was huddled on the roof. "I feel like we're missing out on the best part of the mission being up here."

Geroux ignored him and fiddled with her wrist computer, setting up a program to alert her if anyone tried to exit through the heavily-guarded back gateway. It automatically used her advanced optics to keep watch, so she settled in beside the Melowi, ready for a long wait.

"I need to sit down with my uncle and build some small cloak-enabled drones for this kind of boring grunt work," Geroux muttered. "They'd be perfect for a low-tech world like this one. No one would ever see them."

"Sign me up," Asya said with a grin. "At least when I'm stuck on the ship, there are things to do. Out here in the field on babysitting duty, there's nothing to do but pick your nose and decide where to wipe it."

Geroux laughed. "How ladylike."

"You start to get creative after a while," Asya said, grinning.

"This one time—" Ka'nak started, miming wiping his hand on something, but a sensor went off inside Geroux's helmet, thankfully cutting the demonstration short.

Geroux bolted upright and focused in on the warning. She spotted the emperor's sister approaching the mass of guards on the far side of the building.

"Aht Gow's on the move," Geroux announced, pointing toward where the emperor's sister had emerged from the compound.

"So is the crew," Asya replied, tapping Geroux and Ka'nak on their shoulders to draw their attention to where Asya was looking.

Geroux saw the crew, the emperor, and a number of guards creep out of the very building they were posted on.

"How the hell did they get in there?" Ka'nak grunted, clambering to his feet.

"I don't know, but their timing fucking sucks," Asya growled. *What's going on?* she asked Jiya over the mental link.

Don't know yet, Jiya answered. *Emperor wants some serious privacy for some reason we haven't learned yet. Stick to the mission. We'll figure things out on our end and update you when we know something.*

"I don't care what she says, we need to go after them," Ka'nak stated. "This is strange, them traipsing after this guy."

"We need to follow the sister, too, though," Geroux muttered, torn between helping her crew and following her orders.

It didn't look as if the crew were in trouble, seeing as how they were still in their armor and traveling with the emperor. Also, Jiya hadn't said anything to indicate they were worried, but it was clear they were being stealthy, staying out of sight of the average citizens and the guards at the compound.

Something was going on.

"I guess we're splitting up," Geroux grumbled.

Asya nodded. "Who do you want?"

"Ka'nak's better qualified to deal with a physical threat, so I'd say he should go after the crew and the emperor and keep them safe. You and I can follow the sister and see what's going on with her."

Ka'nak agreed without argument. "On it," he replied,

giving them a thumbs-up and starting off. He was always ready for action.

Before Geroux could respond, Ka'nak dropped off the far side of the building where the crew had emerged and started after them, cloaking himself before he hit the ground.

Geroux grunted at his abrupt departure, but she was grateful Takal had designed the crew's suit optics to be able to see the cloaked members so they could keep track of each other. She watched Ka'nak until he vanished around a corner.

"Just us, I guess," she told Asya.

"Yup. Let's do this," Asya said, patting Geroux on the back for encouragement.

The pair triggered their cloaking devices and raced off after the emperor's sister.

They circled around the compound and caught up with Aht Gow as she left the guard station. The female strolled regally down the barren walk, chin up, back straight, as one would expect of royalty, but that all changed a few moments later.

Once Aht Gow was out of sight of the guards, she bolted down a confined alley.

Asya and Geroux ran after her. Geroux stopped at the corner and peeked around. She spotted her, and was surprised to see her pulling a sandy-brown robe out from under her dress. Geroux hadn't realized she'd been carrying anything.

Aht Gow slipped the robe on, hiding both her sash and dress beneath it, and wrapped a cloth around her head, effectively disguising herself.

Had Geroux not seen her change clothes, she might not have realized that the person she had followed into the alley was the same one who exited the far end.

Sneaky, Geroux thought.

She glanced back at Asya, who stood there studying the female they were following.

The fact that Aht Gow had disguised herself only added to Geroux's distrust. They'd already determined she was up to something, but the quick-change act made it clear Reynolds had made the right choice by keeping an eye out for her.

Now, they needed to figure out where she was going and what she was up to.

Even cloaked, however, the task wasn't easy.

Aht Gow strolled out onto the walkway at the end of the alley and quickly joined the crowd of passersby that congregated there, blending in.

Geroux had missed some signal that stirred the populace into motion, since it seemed the whole of Ulf came alive right then.

People poured out of the shops and homes all at once and joined the already substantial gathering on the walks, the overflow spilling onto the streets.

Asya cursed under her breath as the pair were forced to dodge the citizens wandering about while tracking Aht Gow.

Now would be a damn good time for that drone, Geroux complained.

She caught snippets of conversations as the emperor's sister wound her way through the crowd. Apparently, the end of the workday had been called and everyone was returning home, which left Geroux and Asya struggling against the tide of tired workers looking forward to returning to their families and relaxing.

Aht Gow had used this ploy before.

She weaved in and out of the crowd with ease, looking no different than any of the other non-Muultu surrounding her. Geroux noted there were more of them than she'd initially thought.

The pair nearly lost sight of the emperor's sister several times in the crowd, but either Asya or Geroux always managed to catch up and mark her before she slipped away.

It wasn't until the female veered off and started up a steep hill toward some stone buildings on a rise that towered above the area of the city they'd been traveling through that the foot traffic began to clear.

About damn time, Geroux growled, speeding up to get closer. Asya raced alongside her.

They went on for a while, and Geroux was impressed by Aht Gow's composure. She strolled along as if she belonged among the common people.

Her regal saunter was gone, replaced by a work-weary lope that copied the walks of the people surrounding her. She nodded to them now and again, a quick and noncommittal gesture, but she never said anything or stopped, always remaining on the move.

It wasn't until they neared the top of the hill that she slowed noticeably.

Aht Gow set a pace that kept her behind a small group of people, and then, when they were comfortably far enough ahead to not know she was there, the emperor's sister shot into a narrow crack between the tall walls of the two nearest estates.

Geroux bit back a curse. She wasn't sure they could follow the female, given the armored suits they wore.

She came up on the space and glanced between the walls, glad to realize there was just enough room for the two of them to squeeze through one behind the other.

Aht Gow had reached the middle of the makeshift alley by then and slipped out of sight. Not wanting to lose her, Geroux bolted into the tiny space, Asya right on her heels.

They found where Aht Gow had turned off and caught sight of her opening a small metal gate that led into the estate to the right. The gate clanked shut behind her and Geroux crept up to it, peering through the crack between the metal gate and the wall.

A small courtyard lay beyond, cast in shadows by the twelve-foot walls that surrounded it. Three males stood guard within, rifles of some kind in their hands.

Geroux didn't recognize that type of weapons, although she realized they were mechanical, not the blasters she and the crew were armed with. She didn't think they could hurt her or Asya, but she erred on the side of caution and kept from drawing attention to either of them.

Can't hurt to be smart.

Geroux held up a hand to keep Asya from getting too close and raised three fingers to indicate how many people were there.

She kicked herself mentally a second later since she could have engaged the mental link and relayed that information in person.

Subterfuge isn't my thing.

While she watched, Aht Gow greeted one of the men, and he waved her on after she pulled her scarf back and revealed her face. He said something to her that was too low for Geroux to hear, but Aht Gow nodded in reply before climbing the short flight of steps to the side door of the estate. A soldier inside opened the door and let her in.

Geroux inched closer to the crack and focused her advanced optics to look inside before the guard closed the door.

She caught sight of what appeared to be a wealthy home.

Stone and glass decorations abounded; it was the most extravagant place Geroux had seen on the planet so far, not that she'd seen many. But given what the others had reported regarding the spartan palace and guest chambers, she was shocked to see such lavish decorations in the home.

It seemed out of place in the plain, simple world that was Muultar, so it wasn't what she expected.

The guard closed the door behind Aht Gow, blocking Geroux's view. There were small rectangular windows to the sides of the doors, but they were covered by metal slats that prevented her from seeing through them.

Geroux raised her hand as if to ask, "What now?"

We need to see if we can get a look inside, Asya told her over the link. *And one of us needs to get up on the roof and keep an eye out.*

How do we do that? Geroux asked.

Asya pointed to the wall.

Although it was tall, Geroux could see that the top had been shaped in a way to provide a makeshift ledge. Her gaze followed it around, and she realized it encircled the whole of the house, providing a path around the entire estate.

She turned back to Asya, who held her hands cupped in front of her, expecting Geroux to step into them and slither up the wall.

Geroux drew a deep breath and nodded her agreement. She cast a glance in the guards' direction through the crack and waited until they were looking away before stepping into Asya's hands.

Asya lifted her without effort, doing it slowly to keep quiet, and Geroux clambered onto the narrow ledge on top of the wall.

Once she was settled and had made sure the guards hadn't noticed, she turned around and stretched out a hand to Asya, helping her up the wall.

The pair started off, skirting the edge with slow, patient steps to keep from toppling off or making noise.

There was no doubt that the wall would hold them. Everything was built to extreme standards using the most robust materials.

As they closed on the part of the wall nearest the house, Asya jumped across, landing gracefully on the roof.

There was a muffled *thump* and both Asya and Geroux froze in place, holding their breath. Several moments passed before either exhaled.

No one came out to check or opened a window to look.

I'll go up and take a look at what's around us, Asya said. *You find a window that's open and see if you can locate Aht Gow.*

Geroux accepted the plan and continued along the wall while Asya patrolled the roof. On the other side of the house, Geroux found a window where the slats had been left open.

She hunkered down to peer inside despite the awkward angle. At first, she couldn't see much more than the house's décor, as she had through the door earlier, but a flash of movement caught her eye.

The emperor's sister paced back and forth in an empty room, threatening to wear a groove in the stone tiles. Her scarf off, Aht Gow looked frustrated, or maybe nervous, Geroux thought.

She wasn't the self-assured royal who had strolled casually away from the compound earlier.

We've got company up front, Asya reported a moment later. *Oh...shit.*

What is it? Geroux fired back.

I think we've found our smoking blaster, Asya replied. *You have eyes on the sister?*

I do. What's going on?

You'll see in a minute, Asya responded, refusing to say more.

Geroux growled at the non-revelation. Aht Gow stiffened and stopped pacing, drawing her attention. The emperor's sister turned and looked at the doorway as it opened and Geroux saw what Asya had been referring to.

A male entered the room, and if anyone could be considered a stereotypical cult member, this guy was him.

Dressed in long robes like the Phraim-'Eh devotees she'd seen on Krokus 1 and 4, the cultist carried himself with the same brand of arrogance. He moved as if he expected the world to step out of his way, and Geroux was shocked to see that even Aht Gow deferred to him.

She bowed her head as he approached, and he laid a hand on the top of it. He said something, but there was no way Geroux could hear what it was.

The emperor's sister raised her head once the man's hand was gone. She looked flushed, almost awed by the contact.

He wasn't a Muultu, his skin showing no signs of the scarred and ravaged flesh that was indicative of the natives. His skin was pale almost to the point of gleaming and he was without hair of any kind, either on his head or face.

The cultist looked as withered and aged as if he'd been alive for thousands of years, yet there was an obvious vitality to him that belied the presumption. His eyes were gleaming black orbs.

Geroux attuned her suit's senses to try to hear what was going on, but the nature of the atmosphere or the house or some unknown device—or all three—kept her from hearing the conversation.

She cursed under her breath and did her best to read their lips, but their interchange was short-lived. The cultist seemed to almost bark at Aht Gow, poking a finger in front of her face.

The emperor's sister flinched with every jab.

The pseudo-conversation lasted all of a minute before the cultist reached out and handed Aht Gow a device Geroux thought she recognized.

A computer?

The cultist said one last thing to Aht Gow and spun on his heel, his robes flowing around him as he stormed from the room. The emperor's sister nearly collapsed once he was gone, clutching the device.

He's headed back your way, Geroux told Asya. *I don't know what went on between the two of them, but it was heated. And he gave her some kind of device. Think it's a computer.*

Asya growled over the link. *What the hell's going on here?*

I don't know, but the sister is powering up the device. I'm going to see if I can break through the resistance on this house and try and hack it. See what she's up to, Geroux said.

The cultist is leaving, Asya reported. *Damn it. There's no time to do both without losing one or the other.*

Geroux sighed. *Guess we're splitting up again.*

Looks that way, Asya replied. *Go ahead and do what you have to here, but don't get caught,* she warned. *I'm going to follow our cult-dick. Maybe he'll lead me to Phraim-'Eh or Jora'nal.*

Stay safe, she called to Asya before the connection went silent.

Geroux looked back through the window. Aht Gow had powered up the device and had begun tapping at its console. Geroux followed suit and opened her wrist computer.

There's no way some backwater security is going to keep me from seeing what's on that device.

Geroux snarled and got to work, pecking at her wrist console.

CHAPTER SEVEN

Ka'nak caught up to the crew a few moments after they'd departed, as the emperor led them through darkened and shadowy alleys off the main thoroughfare.

As he turned the corner and saw them, he realized he'd caught them just in time.

A guard surveyed the area behind the group suspiciously and went to the wall in a dead-end alley they'd entered. Ka'nak zoomed in with his optics and watched what the guard did as the wall swung open to reveal a hidden entrance to the building.

He waited until everyone had gone inside and the door had closed before going to the wall and taking a closer look.

The mechanism that kept the door locked was inventive, but with the advanced tech of his suit and knowing exactly where to look for the abnormality, it stood out against the otherwise plain wall.

He could see how it would be invisible to someone without his technological advantages, though.

Ka'nak waited a few moments, listening as best he could to make sure no one was standing on the other side of the fake wall before he triggered the mechanism and stepped inside after the others.

Darkness greeted him, and his suit adjusted to the lighting, the tiny room arrayed before him. It was a meter wide and three meters long at most.

Another secret doorway secured the far end of the room, the same type of device used to lock it.

Ka'nak went over to it and listened once more, hearing nothing. He sucked in a deep breath and opened the second door, finding a steep, narrow stairwell on the other side.

He eased down the stairs and arrived in what appeared to be a kind of sewer system, moisture dripping from the walls and ceiling. A tiny river of muck spilled from a massive pipe and ran down the slight incline toward an unknown destination. A slim walkway skirted the refuse water and disappeared into the distance.

It was the only way to go from there, plus, when he turned up the acoustics on his suit, he could hear the shuffling of feet in that direction.

Ka'nak sighed, glad that his helmet filtered out the smell of whatever was floating in the water. He had no doubt he had smelled worse, having been raised in the stink of the gladiatorial pits, but that didn't mean he liked or wanted to smell it.

He started off after the footsteps, wondering what he, the emperor, and the crew were getting into.

He didn't have long to wait.

Ka'nak drew close enough to see the rest of the group as they came to yet another dead-end. Once again, the soldier manipulated something on the wall and ushered them inside, closing the door behind them after they were all through.

Ka'nak went to the wall and triggered the same mechanism, making sure to barely crack the door rather than let it swing open wide.

While he wasn't the best of the crew at stealthy maneuvers, he'd had enough experience sneaking around that he knew better than to rush in and leave himself and his crew exposed.

He eased against the wall and peered through the smallest of cracks between the wall and secret door, letting his visor adjust and give him a better view.

The room looked like a factory of some kind, and Ka'nak recognized the same material stacked around the place that Jiya had brought back in the damaged Pod.

He stared as Reynolds and the crew gathered around.

The guards moved off and took up posts around the room, giving Reynolds and the emperor space to talk without the soldiers being right on top of them.

The chamber they'd entered was massive. While simplistic, the level of tech barely effective, the room rumbled with a system of conveyor belts and devices that appeared to be processing the devium in bulk.

The ore was fed through machines that ground it into a powder and then transported to another machine that appeared to irradiate it before sending it along to the next, which filled a mobile containment box before it was wheeled away on tracks.

Krol Gow raised his arms and gestured around the room. "This is our devium processing plant."

Reynolds didn't know if the emperor was bragging or complaining, so the AI simply nodded in reply.

"This ore is what fuels the atmospheric boundary that holds out the majority of Muultar's toxic air and keeps ours breathable," Krol Gow explained. "It's also the primary energy source for our vehicles and spacecraft."

Reynolds glanced around the room again and realized that many of the machines in the back of the room were silent. Very little ore was being processed at the moment.

"Is production always so…slow?" Reynolds asked.

The emperor sighed. "That is why I have brought you here," he admitted. "When Takal," he gestured to the old inventor and smiled, "spoke of your ship's capabilities, I felt I had found the means to an end."

"You want us to do something for you," Jiya realized. "That's why we're here."

"I do indeed." The emperor nodded. "In exchange for your assistance in this matter, I will provide you and your crew the safe haven you requested, as well as supplies when you pass through our system in the future."

"And if we decide not to help?" Reynolds asked, curious to see what the emperor's response would be.

Krol Gow checked to make sure the guards were outside hearing range, and he sighed. "If you choose to refuse my request, it is quite likely that there will no longer be a Muultar for you to visit," he answered. "The planet will remain for a time, but there will be no one alive to assist you with your needs."

"What do you mean?" Maddox asked.

"Before I go on, I must swear all of you to secrecy," Krol Gow stated. "I cannot have word of this reaching the populace. There would be chaos, and many people would die. Do you agree?"

Reynolds nodded. "We do."

The emperor hesitated for a moment as if questioning Reynolds' word before he went on, "Our supply of devium is at an end, I'm afraid," he told them. "Until recently, perhaps a year ago, we were able to mine a nearby planet in our system. Uninhabited, it is registered as MU-2693, though we've always referred to it as 'Mu.'"

He pronounced it as if he were mimicking an Earth cow.

"What's happened?" Takal asked.

"A powerful race of alien beings has claimed the planet and will not allow us anywhere near it," the emperor went on. "They arrived one day without warning and destroyed four of our cruisers and numerous transport ships. That has left us scraping the asteroids for the remnants of devium that those old, destroyed worlds once possessed just to maintain our barriers and fuel our machines."

"You can't challenge them with your remaining cruisers?" Maddox asked, eyes narrowed.

The emperor shook his head. "Our technology is simple, as you have no doubt seen. The ships we had orbiting Mu were wiped out in moments by a single craft of the several they appear to possess. Our people weren't even given an opportunity to fight back. Only a single transport escaped to report what had happened. We don't stand a chance against such ferocity, and we no longer have the energy supply to expend upon the effort.

"To be blunt, our ships are little more than a deterrent to outside forces to warn them away. A bluff, if you will."

"But you think we have the firepower to take these guys on?" Reynolds stared at the emperor, trying to see if the Muultu believed what he was saying.

It appeared he did. He looked downright forlorn at the prospect that Reynolds would refuse to help.

"I can only hope, Reynolds," Krol Gow replied somberly. "We have no other option but to hope someone can chase the aliens from the planet so we can return to mining the devium." He sighed and leaned against the nearest machine. "We are incapable of transporting our people off the planet, and even if our ships were sufficient to the task or we had the fuel, where would we go? We have no FTL drives or Gate technology, as Takal described it, and no one would take on over two million Muultu."

Reynolds stood there for a moment, contemplating what the emperor was telling him. Even if the SD *Reynolds* assisted and carried the people off the planet, it would take forever. There were simply too many, discounting the fact that there was nowhere to drop off two million alien beings. No established civilization would take that many, and Reynolds couldn't set aside his mission long enough to find sufficient worlds for everyone.

It was clear why the emperor had been so friendly to them; so confiding. He was desperate, and there was nothing he could do to extricate his people from the impending disaster.

"Have you attempted to speak with the aliens?" Jiya asked, although it was clear from her expression that she was simply running the problem through and already had a good idea what the answer was.

"They reject all attempts at communications," Krol Gow explained. "As far as we know, they didn't even attempt to contact our ships before they destroyed them."

"Can you give us a moment to discuss this among ourselves?" Reynolds asked the emperor.

Krol Gow nodded. "Of course."

He joined his soldiers as the crew gathered around so no one could overhear them. He chose not to use the internal comm so as not to reveal that they had they had a way to communicate privately

Jiya whistled, making a face that told Reynolds her thoughts.

"You don't think we should help them?" Reynolds asked.

She shook her head. "No, I definitely think we should *try* to help them," she answered without hesitation. "I'm just not sure we can. This alien race wiped out four of their cruisers in an instant."

Maddox shrugged. "Well, their ships aren't exactly world beaters. The *Reynolds* could take them out as easily."

"That's kind of my point," Jiya went on. "That means we're likely dealing with another superdreadnought, or more likely several of them, seeing as how that's what Krol Gow said. That's a lot of firepower to take on, even for the *Reynolds*."

"She's not incorrect," Takal agreed.

"We're just guessing here, though," Reynolds added.

"Which is why I said we should *try* to help," Jiya continued. "I know you're willing to go out of your way to help the people of these planets we come across, and that's a good thing, but correct me if I'm wrong: we can't lay aside your Kurtherian mission to fight other people's battles against an enemy we can't beat, right?"

Reynolds was torn. He knew Jiya was correct, that the mission he'd been set upon was what was important, but he took a moment to think about Bethany Anne and what she would tell him about this situation.

He chuckled, imagining her response.

"Bethany Anne is a believer in Justice," he stated. "While she would be pissed if we threw away our lives and assets in a futile fight, she would just as quickly put her foot up my metallic ass for walking away from people who are downtrodden and need our help.

"Were I to ask her what she thought, she would no doubt say something creatively crude and vulgar I couldn't possibly mimic and then she would tell us to do what's right, simple as that."

"So, that means we're going to evict these aliens?" Maddox asked.

"We'll surveil them first," Reynolds countered, "because Bethany Anne would also turn me into scrap if I went off and did something dumb for no reason other than trying to make her happy."

"I haven't met her, but I already like her." Jiya laughed.

"As do I," Reynolds admitted, "but she wouldn't want us putting ourselves at risk for something stupid or as an empty gesture where we just get ourselves killed. We need to find out what we're up against and we can go from there. Maybe we can negotiate something with these aliens, whoever they are. It could be that the Muultu are too simplistic to have recognized communications from them."

"Or they could be hostile bastards who want to see everyone burn," Maddox added.

"That is another possibility," Reynolds agreed. "I guess we'll find out soon enough. Information will be our friend, and we'll gather as much of it as we can."

The AI signaled the emperor that they were done discussing the issue. Krol Gow returned quickly, staring at the crew with expectant eyes.

"I make no promises, Emperor," Reynolds started, "since we have no idea what we will be facing or how we match up against these aliens you speak of. However, we will do what we can."

The emperor seemed to deflate as he let out a deep breath. "Thank you, Reynolds. I can ask for no more than that."

"We'll travel to Mu, see what we can see, and determine our course of action from there," Reynolds explained. "I do, however, want something more than simply a safe haven and supplies should we succeed."

The emperor stiffened at that, but he nodded regardless. "If you release us from our dilemma, you have only to name it."

"Then we're off to see what we can do for you and your people, Emperor." Reynolds extended his hand, and Krol Gow clasped it in agreement.

After they shook hands, the emperor and his guards led the crew back to the hidden door.

Reynolds caught sight of it easing closed before they arrived, and he grinned. Once the door was open, he ushered the crew and soldiers ahead of him, trailing behind the group a short distance without anyone noticing.

He caught movement out of the corner of his eye, and a shape rose out of the water at their backs.

Nice to know you care enough to follow us, Ka'nak, but shouldn't you be elsewhere? Reynolds asked over the mental link.

Looked like you might need help, the Melowi answered. *Figured I'd follow you while the ladies chased down the emperor's sister.*

I suspect you overhead our conversation from your post at the door?

I did, Ka'nak admitted. *Guess we're headed out to blow some folks up.*

Just us, Reynolds told him. *I want you to go back and assist Geroux and Asya while we're gone. They'll need your raw talents more than we will.*

I wish you'd told me that before I jumped in the sewer water to hide. Ka'nak groaned. *I sure could use a good hosing off.*

The AI chuckled. *I'm sure you'll figure out something. Stay safe, and protect the crew here on Muultar. We'll return as soon as possible.*

Reynolds left the Melowi behind and caught back up with the crew as the emperor led them out of the secret devium factory.

He didn't know what he was getting himself or the crew into, but he suspected they'd appreciate him leaving the smelly warrior behind.

CHAPTER EIGHT

"I feel weird. It's like we're abandoning them," Jiya complained when they were once more on the bridge of the SD *Reynolds*. "I don't like it."

She was sitting in the vacated captain's chair where Asya should have been, and she twisted uncomfortably. Jiya had no issue going after the aliens who had cut off the Muultu's energy source, but she didn't appreciate leaving her people—her friends—behind.

"They're safer there than we are, I suspect," Reynolds told her bluntly.

"Oh, now I feel better," she snarked. "Thanks for that."

"If that's the case, you can fucking leave me behind, too," Tactical told them. "I don't care if you're suicidal, but I'm not, you ragweed-sniffing butt-stain!"

"Now, now, Tactical. Some decorum, please. You know this side mission is what Bethany Anne would want," Reynolds shot back.

"I'm sure she would want me to live. She always liked me better than you," Tactical returned. "Besides, you've got legs, asshole. You can walk your ass to the fight if you're looking to make a last stand against some monstrous aliens."

"No one's dying, damn it!" Jiya cursed. "Stop saying that!"

"What crawled up your ass and bit it?" Tactical asked.

"A splintered AI with delusions of independence," she snapped. She wasn't in the mood for Tactical's bullshit.

"Ouch!" Comm laughed. "Fire at Tactical's position. AI down! Medic!"

"ORDER," Reynolds roared at a volume which caused those with ears to cover them. "We're on a surveillance mission first and foremost, reaching out to these aliens to figure out who they are and what they want in the system. We're not looking for a fight, but if they want one, we'll give them more than they can handle."

"And what are we getting by putting our asses on the line for these people?" Tactical asked.

"The emperor's cooperation in finding out what his sister knows about the Phraim-'Eh cult," Reynolds answered.

"I thought that was what Geroux and Asya were doing," Maddox said.

"They are, but it doesn't hurt to come at the problem more than one way," the AI told him. "I believe Krol Gow is ignorant of what's happening on Muultar, but I've no doubt he can apply enough pressure to help us find out what Phraim-'Eh's cultists are doing behind the scenes with his people. There were too many of them helping that Jora'nal scab to be a coincidence."

Reynolds motioned to Ensign Alcott. "Set a course for

Mu. Stations, people. Sound General Quarters. Battlestations."

"Mu to you too, buddy," Tactical mumbled as the ship became a flurry of activity.

"All systems are green. All hands confirmed at battlestations," XO announced.

"Course set," Ria remarked. "Gate activated."

Jiya clasped the arms of the captain's chair and drew in a deep breath. There was good reason to question the emperor's intel, since it had come secondhand through a source that had barely escaped with their life.

There was no telling how accurate the information was, but the man's conviction was enough to make Jiya worry about what they were Gating into.

He had seemed so sure these aliens were unbeatable.

"Shields at one hundred percent. On our way," Ria reported as the ship moved into the event horizon.

Jiya trusted Reynolds and the superdreadnought was a monster of a ship, able to handle almost anything. She'd just learned the hard way that their mission was a dangerous one.

She wanted to help the Muultu, she just wanted to do it safely.

"Through the gate," Ria announced.

Jiya settled into her seat, calming her nerves. Being antsy wouldn't help. She knew her duty, knew what the SD *Reynolds* was capable of, trusted the crew, and understood what its captain could do.

Nothing could stand in their way.

"Mu dead ahead," Ria called out.

"Got milk?" Tactical asked.

"Can we shut him off?" Jiya asked.

"You wish," Tactical replied.

"I *so* do," she muttered as XO brought the planet up on the screen.

Jiya gasped when she saw it.

"It's beautiful."

The orb was a soft blue, with sections of white at the poles. It had an interesting swirl of clouds that moved leisurely across its surface, drawing her eye as if they were a work of art.

Above it loomed a large moon that appeared to reflect the light from the planet rather than from its distant suns. It gleamed a brilliant teal color and looked as if it were a giant eye, staring down at the planet below.

"How is it that this place can look like this, and Muultu looks ready to explode, and that's where all the people are?" Maddox asked.

"Because this planet is outside of the habitable zone," XO explained. "All that blue you're seeing isn't water, but rather a toxic mix of hydrogen and helium that makes up the atmosphere."

"I guess that means the aliens don't breathe air," Jiya suggested.

Reynolds shrugged. "Could be they aren't on the surface. Conduct a long-range scan, Ensign. Find out what and who all is here with us."

"On it, sir," Ria replied, fingers tapping her console.

The crew spent a few quiet moments admiring the view of the planet, only to be interrupted by Ria announcing they had incoming.

"We've got a ship rising from the planet's atmosphere, sir," Ria warned.

"What have we got, Tactical?" Reynolds asked. "Kurtherian?"

"Definitely not Kurtherian, but I don't know what the hell that thing is," Tactical said. "The readings I'm getting back are telling me it's packing serious power, though. We need to be careful."

Reynolds brought the ship up on the screen. The bridge crew examined it closely as the camera zoomed in.

"That doesn't look like something humanoids would fit in comfortably," the first officer commented. "It looks…odd."

"Its shields are up, and weapons primed," Tactical called.

"Hail it, Comm," Reynolds ordered. "Keep us at a safe distance, Ensign, but in a position to return fire if need be."

"All I'm getting back is gibberish," Comm complained. "It doesn't seem like any language I've ever heard. If they're answering our hails, I don't have a clue what they're saying."

"Damn it!" Reynolds snarled. "Find another way to let them know we're not here for a fight."

There was a flash of energy from the alien ship and an impact on the SD *Reynolds'* shields an instant later.

The ship trembled, and Jiya clasped her seat to keep from being thrown off.

"Son of a badger's ass," Reynolds shouted. "Sitrep?"

"Big bad guy just spanked us for entering his space," Tactical reported.

"Anyone else?" Reynolds ordered.

"That was one hell of a hit," XO replied. "There's no classification on it, but I'm guessing it's as much a super-dreadnought as we are."

"No one's as super as you guys are," Jiya said. "Hit them back, Tactical."

"My pleasure."

Tactical returned fire, letting loose with the railguns, and peppered the enemy ship with high-velocity rounds that flashed as they struck their shields and slammed into the hull.

"Got him!" Tactical shouted. "Take that, asshole."

"Looks like they took it fine," XO reported, examining the damage reports coming in. "They've got some holes in their hull now, but it's not slowing them down. They're returning fire."

"Evasive maneuvers," Reynolds ordered.

Ria complied instantly, but several bursts of energy crashed into the gravitic shields and set the ship shuddering.

Some of the blasts had gotten through to impact the ship itself. Red warning lights bathed the bridge, sirens wailing.

"Damage report," Reynolds requested.

"They punched a hole in our aft compartments, but auto-systems are handling it. The section is sealed, and we're not venting atmosphere. Bots are responding to rein-force the repairs," XO stated.

"No injuries...yet," Jiya reported.

"Hitting him with everything," Tactical announced.

The SD *Reynolds* continued to evade return fire as Tactical unleashed hell on the enemy ship. Sparks erupted as the barrage tore through the alien shields and exploded against the hull.

The ship started to list and debris littered the space around the wound, but there was no indication of venting.

"I think we got our answer as to whether these bastards breathe air," Maddox called. "We jabbed a couple of holes in their armor, but I'm not seeing any atmospheric interruption."

"Keep hitting them with everything you've got, Tactical," Reynolds commanded.

The *Reynolds* swung about since the enemy ship seemed determined to come straight at them without bothering to adjust its flight path in response to the weapons fire it was receiving.

"And here I thought *you* were the suicidal one," Tactical told the AI. "These guys are coming straight at us like they're playing a game of chicken."

"Their shield levels have just doubled," XO spat.

"Speed's increasing," Ria warned, her voice cracking on the last. "They're coming right at us."

The enemy ship streaked past the starboard side faster than Jiya imagined a ship could move, weapons strafing the *SD Reynolds*.

The ship bucked, and it took all of Jiya's strength to remain seated. She felt the superdreadnought start to roll and heard Reynolds growl as Ria fought to right the ship. The ensign managed it a moment later.

"Shields are down to forty percent," Jiya reported, amazed they hadn't taken more damage from that latest attack run.

"They're ripping us a new one," Tactical cursed.

"I kind of like the old one the way it is," Reynolds replied. "Ready the ESD and bring us about to face them."

"Who the hell *are* these fuckers?" XO asked.

"No time for questions, XO," Reynolds told him. "Just get ready to swat them out of space."

"They're coming back around," Ria announced.

"Already?" Reynolds asked, unable to believe how quickly the enemy ship maneuvered.

"ESD coming online, but it's not going to be fast enough, Captain," Tactical warned. "You sure you want to fire this thing, seeing what it does to our systems? This ship is too damn fast to risk leaving us flailing out here."

Hearing Tactical warn against using the ESD—the Eat Shit and Die beam—made her blood run cold.

Normally, he was the first one to suggest the weapon, which fired the equivalent of a solar flare, taking out damn near everything that stood in its way.

Well, now that they'd figured out the glitch that had sapped its power when they'd used it against Jora'nal and the *Pillar*, it did.

"You have any better ideas?" Reynolds demanded.

Tactical lit up the approaching ship with everything he had in his arsenal except for the ESD, which was still powering up.

The enemy ship streaked past as the two superdreadnoughts exchanged fire.

The lights on the bridge dimmed as explosions impacted the length of the SD *Reynolds*. Warning beacons flashed on Jiya's console and across all stations, and a low rumble sounded throughout the ship and lingered. Black smoke clouded the bridge, growing thicker despite the life support systems' efforts to clear it out.

"Shields are almost gone," Jiya reported once she was able to wave the smoke away from her console and see it clearly. "Damage reports incoming. Fires on several decks and multiple hull breaches. There are...oh, fuck!"

"Report, First Officer," Reynolds demanded.

Jiya choked in a deep breath and spat the words out. "We've got casualties. Five dead, twenty-three wounded. Wait, six dead."

Reynolds snarled. "We do anything to those mother-fuckers?"

"We've hurt them but it's not slowing them down," Tactical answered.

"We can't penetrate their hull with scanners, so we don't know if they've sustained any casualties on their end," XO reported.

"Or if they even care whether they have," Reynolds spat out. "The ESD up?"

"Ten seconds," Tactical told him.

"They're coming around again," Ria said.

"Their shields have doubled again," XO stated, awe in his voice. "How are they doing that?"

"Can we get past them?" Reynolds asked.

Jiya could hear the uncertainty in XO's voice.

"I don't know," he answered. "I've never seen a ship like this one before."

"They're coming at us, sir," Ria called. She managed to keep her voice steady, but there was no hiding the ghostly pallor of her skin.

She was terrified.

"Let them get close—" Reynolds started.

"As if we have a choice," Tactical interrupted, growling the words.

"—and roll the shields to coincide with their attack locations."

Jiya clung to her seat as the enemy ship shot past once again, firing its payload at nearly point-blank range.

XO did as ordered and pulled all the energy into the shields, triggering them in a ripple effect that shunted as much energy as possible into each impact point as the enemy ship hurtled past.

Jiya held her breath as the *Reynolds* shook under the assault.

"It worked," XO shouted.

"Mostly," Jiya countered, watching more damage reports roll across her screen.

Ten more of their crew had died in the attack, and the numbers were rising.

"ESD at minimal power!" Tactical alerted.

"About fucking time," Reynolds snarled. "These wanksplats have stuck to the exact same course on every maneuver, so target these coordinates and let them eat shit."

Reynolds transmitted the coordinates to Tactical, who used them to target the enemy ship.

Sure enough, the aliens did exactly as they had done previously, swinging around in the same manner as before, opening themselves up to a counterstrike.

Tactical let loose with the ESD, and the power on the bridge dimmed to almost nothing. The viewscreen flared with blinding illumination as the burst of energy streaked across space and bulls-eyed the turning enemy craft.

There was a surge as the shields gave way and the ESD tore into the ship.

The enemy superdreadnought was thrown sideways as a large chunk of its stern was ripped away, sent tumbling into space in an ever-expanding debris cloud.

The viewscreen flickered and went black, coming back on a few seconds later as the *Reynolds'* system rebooted. The consoles were slow to return, but Jiya finally managed to get hers back online.

"They're incapacitated," XO reported , a victorious growl in his voice.

"Once the guns are back up, grind that ship to dust," Reynolds ordered. "Move us into position, Ensign. Comm, make sure they get a graphically-detailed message telling them what we're going to do to their asses now."

Jiya was still checking the damage reports, trying to get an accurate account of all the people who'd lost their lives in the fight, when she picked up a signal on the scanners. A second appeared right after.

Her heart froze in her chest.

"We need to get the fuck out of here *now!*" she shrieked, not giving a damn how she sounded.

"We're not leaving until we—" Reynolds started, but Helm asserted control and the SD *Reynolds'* engines engaged. The ship shot off, veering away from the wrecked hulk of the enemy ship.

Reynolds spun with a growl, not sure who to focus his fury on, but Maddox's words stopped him in his tracks.

"Two more of the enemy ships have broken out of the

Mu atmosphere and are tracking us," the general warned. Reynolds wondered about the wisdom of blocking his higher functions from those of the ship, which was also Reynolds. He would have instantly known and had the Gate drive spooling up.

Reynolds spun back around and looked at the screen showing the two ships, identical to the first, streaking toward the *Reynolds*.

The burning vengeance on his face had cooled, and the AI took personal control and set a course that carried the ship away from Mu. He opened a Gate as soon as the ship had the energy to do so.

Without a word, he piloted the ship through the Gate as the enemy craft closed, then cut the Gate drive immediately once they were through, sealing the portal behind them.

"Drop mines," he ordered as he opened yet another Gate and shot into it, transporting the superdreadnought across the system, leaving a swath of deadly presents behind.

Two more Gates and dozens of mines later, Reynolds brought the ship to a halt so they could accurately assess the damage they'd suffered in the battle.

All in all, they'd lost twenty-five of the crew, and there were over a hundred people injured. Jiya slumped in her seat, sickened by the casualty count, but she didn't let her sorrow stop her from doing her job.

"Get the Pod-docs up and running and get our injured in them immediately, most critical first," she ordered over the comm.

"Already underway," Medical Reynolds replied.

Dozens of section reports followed in a wash of noise, and she sent the bots to help ferry the wounded to the med-bay, supporting the crew as much as possible.

There wasn't much more she could do, but she couldn't help herself. She jumped out of her seat.

"Maddox, you have the chair," she called. "Help Reynolds with whatever he needs. I need to get to sickbay."

She didn't wait to see if Reynolds had anything to say, she simply ran off the bridge toward Medical.

CHAPTER NINE

Asya followed the cultist from the estate in upper Ulf, staying cloaked as he covered his head like Aht Gow had done and made his way across town.

He had five others with him, dressed similarly, and none of the casual bystanders gave them more than a cursory glance as they passed in silence. Asya hadn't seen their faces to determine if they were Muultu or of a different alien race.

The streets had returned to their previous lack of traffic, everyone having largely returned home, and the walkways were sparse compared to how they had been when Asya and Geroux had followed the emperor's sister to the estate.

Now it was much easier to trail the cultist and keep from stumbling into anyone else.

She thought for a while that he would walk forever when, at last, he and his entourage turned off the main thoroughfare and struck off toward the atmospheric barrier on the opposite side of the city where she and the crew had flown in.

What the hell is he doing? she asked, doggedly trailing him.

It wasn't long until she had her answer.

The cultist and his followers strode through the barrier at a place where no one in the nearby city could spot them, and they walked out into the toxic haze that made up the rest of the unprotected planet.

Asya adjusted her suit's life support to be certain it would adequately deal with the maelstrom outside and followed.

A stiff, warm wind buffeted her as she stepped out, and she spied the cultist and his people a short distance ahead.

They had swapped their head scarfs for helmets. They wound their way across the hilly, cracked landscape and disappeared behind a thick outcropping.

Asya cursed and sped up, and just as she arrived at the edge of the hill, she heard an engine rumble to life. Furtively, she glanced around the corner to see the cultists piling into an archaic vehicle that made the one Reynolds and the others had ridden in to the palace look like new tech.

It sputtered and spewed smoke from rear pipes, then shot off across the rough, raw terrain.

"Fucking wonderful," she muttered. "Where's a damn Jonny-Taxi when you need one?"

"I should probably call Reynolds," she joked, starting off after the vehicle, using the resources of her powered armor to keep pace so she didn't lose sight of her target.

"Had I known you were going for a jog, I'd have gone with the damn android," Ka'nak told her over the comm.

She glanced back over her shoulder to see the Melowi warrior running behind her. She slowed a little so he could catch up.

"What the hell are you doing out here?" he asked.

"Chasing bad guys. You?"

"Chasing you, apparently," he told her.

"How'd you find me out here?" she asked.

"I was coming back to figure out where you and Geroux were when you strolled right in front of me," he said. "Lost you for a second when you slipped between some houses, but then caught a flicker of the barrier being penetrated. Figured that was you. Guess I was right. Unfortunately. Now here I am."

"You've got good timing," she told him.

"Not from where I'm standing…er, running," he shot back. "Where's Geroux?"

"She's keeping an eye on the emperor's sister. We followed her to an estate in a fancy part of town, and then the cultist in that vehicle we're tracking showed up."

"So, there are cultists here, huh?"

"Looks that way," she replied. "What happened with Reynolds and the others?"

The two continued to run until the vehicle slowed and eased down a decline. It vanished, but with the dust it was kicking up in its wake, it was easy to follow.

"The planet's on its last legs, according to the emperor," Ka'nak informed her. "Some supposed alien menace has claimed their mining planet, which is why they were skimming the asteroids, which are what's left of one of the system's other planets."

"And Reynolds decided to help," Asya said, not even bothering to make it a question.

"Yup, and he sent me to back you and the kid up while we wait for them to finish being heroes and come back to get us."

"When's that going to be?" she asked.

He shrugged, which looked quite awkward while running.

"Soon as they're done. Whenever that is."

The pair came up to the rise the vehicle had descended and Asya stuttered to a stop, sticking her arm out. Ka'nak stumbled into her extended limb and grunted as she kept him from tumbling off a sharp drop.

Asya dropped to her haunches and stared out across the distance, where the vehicle had also come to a halt. Ka'nak crouched beside her.

"Thanks," he muttered, and she nodded in response.

The cultist and his entourage climbed out of the vehicle outside a short, squat building that reminded Asya of a church of some kind. Built in one of the deep ravines, and made out of the same rock as its surroundings, she imagined the place would be difficult to spot from the air unless someone was right over it.

"What kind of moron builds a church out in the middle of fucking nowhere?" Ka'nak snarled.

"Cultists," she replied.

He shrugged at the answer. "Makes sense, I guess."

"Still, you'd think someone would have noticed these

guys cutting through the barrier at some point and reported this?"

"I try not to think on an empty stomach," Ka'nak informed her, rubbing his belly.

"I wonder how long this has been out here?" she questioned as the cultist and his followers pushed through the door and went inside.

"Maybe a couple of years, at the most," Ka'nak replied. He gestured to the roof of the small building, and Asya zoomed in where he pointed. "You see those cuts across the top there?"

She nodded.

"Those are fresh," he said. "You can still see the raw stone underneath where they cut into it to shape the roof. Had it been out here in this nasty weather a long time, those marks would be worn smooth. You wouldn't be able to see the tool strokes."

"A couple of years is still a long time," she remarked.

"If they're out here all the time." The Melowi waved his hand at the sullen, ugly landscape. "I doubt even these guys spend much time in this dump. I'm *sure* none of the locals do. At least those not connected to these cult fuckers."

Asya realized he was right.

This was the perfect place to hide…

As long as you don't mind being irradiated and having your skin lashed from your bones by the wind.

"I wonder what they're doing in there," Asya said.

She hated that she couldn't see or hear anything that was going on because they were so far from the church, relying on their advanced optics to keep the place in view.

"Let's take a closer look," she told Ka'nak.

"I was afraid you'd say that." He sighed as he got to his feet. "I'm with you, but I'm not running this time."

She chuckled and started off, walking down the same path the vehicle had taken. With sufficient cover to keep them hidden the rest of the way to the church, Asya was glad to slow down. They could get next to it and never once step out into the open.

That was the easy part.

Deciding what to do once they were there was something else entirely.

Geroux cracked the cult house's security not more than a few minutes after she'd identified what they were using to keep her out.

It was a simple firewall designed to keep the communications and energy signature of the estate hidden from the neighbors, but Geroux couldn't for the life of her figure out why they needed it.

It wasn't like Muultar was high-tech enough for anyone to notice the firewall, let alone have the skill to identify or bypass it.

Once Geroux was through the defenses, she realized quickly that the device the emperor's sister was working on was the only one within the range of Geroux's own device.

She went after it with gusto, only to hit a wall.

Geroux growled low in her throat as a new line of defenses popped up when she tried to hack the device.

It was nothing like the firewall.

The technology of the computer was sophisticated and alien, and Geroux struggled against its security.

She peered in through the window, still cloaked and undetectable, and was glad that it was the device that shouldered the whole of the defenses and not Aht Gow. The emperor's sister was ignorant of the device's innate abilities as she worked, oblivious to Geroux's efforts to crack into the computer she was using.

Geroux bared her teeth as she worked, pecking at her wrist console, racing to get past the automated security.

She tried code-cracker after code-cracker, working to identify and break into the device. The entire time, the emperor's sister tapped at her keyboard at a leisurely pace.

As Geroux split her focus between Aht Gow and her computer, she saw the Muultu tap one last key and sit back in her chair.

When Geroux's scanners picked up and identified a surge of energy, she realized the emperor's sister was sending some kind of coded message.

Geroux snatched up the signal and recorded it. Out in the open, she had no issue corralling it, although she could neither stop it nor decrypt it at that point. She'd have to settle for being able to examine it after the fact and hoping it wasn't some sort of signal to set something in motion.

While her computer continued to record the encrypted message, she worked at hacking the device. Its security ebbed and flowed with her efforts, and she was nearly ready to quit when a snippet of code ran across her screen.

She gasped, recognizing the string as the signal cut away.

It was the same coding language the Loranian ship had

used to gain control of Gorad's ships, using them to attack the SD *Reynolds*.

"Oh, hell," she muttered.

There was no way she would be able to crack the device before the emperor's sister shut it down, if at all. The code had eluded even Reynolds when he'd first encountered it, and she didn't think he'd broken its secrets yet.

But it didn't matter right that second.

Just seeing the code had made it clear that Aht Gow was connected to Jora'nal and the Phraim-'Eh cult.

Geroux stiffened.

"Shit!"

She triggered her comm and reached out to Asya.

"Everything okay?" Asya said a few moments later.

"Not really," Geroux told her. "Krol Gow's sister sent out a coded message of some kind."

"To whom?" Asya asked.

Geroux shrugged. "Hell if I know, but it uses the same encryption as the code Jora'nal used to hack Gorad's systems. She shot the stream into space."

"That can't be good."

"My thought exactly," Geroux told her.

As she waited for Asya to respond, Aht Gow closed the device and stood up. She slipped it under her belt, wrapped her scarf around her head, and left the room.

"Damn it," Geroux growled. "She's on the move again."

"Stay with her," Asya said.

"On it."

Geroux climbed to her feet and steadied herself on top of the wall. She then made her way back around to the courtyard behind the house as the emperor's sister exited. She headed for the door that led back to the tiny alley.

Geroux beat her there and slithered down the wall at the same time Aht Gow opened the gate, covering the sound of Geroux's descent.

She followed the female out of the alley and back onto the streets, where she started off again at the casual pace she had adopted on the way there.

Geroux let her get a short distance ahead so she could speak to Asya without being paranoid that Aht Gow could hear her voice, even though she knew the sound didn't travel outside the helmet.

"She's heading back to the palace, it looks like," Geroux reported. "We're following the same path back."

"Uh, you didn't happen to catch what that message said, did you?" Asya asked a moment later.

"I can't be sure because I couldn't crack the code, but I have to assume she was reporting our presence here to someone and calling for help, or maybe warning someone off. Neither of those helps us."

"She was signaling someone," Asya said after a few seconds pause.

Geroux made a face. "How do you know?" she asked.

"Because an alien ship is coming down right on top of us."

***

"This can't be good," Ka'nak complained as he spotted the strange alien craft streaking through the hazy air.

It came about and dropped down less than five meters

away, landing gear thumping on the dusty ground. Its hatch opened as the ship settled, and the strangest life-forms Asya had ever seen emerged from the ship.

"What the fuck are those?" she asked, nearly choking on the words.

The creatures were amorphous blobs of energy that floated out of the ship on what appeared to be tendrils of lightning. They had no discernable features of any kind—no eyes, no ears, nose, or mouth. Nor did they have any limbs.

Their transparent gelatinous forms shimmered and changed shape without rhyme or reason. It looked as if they had nuclear generators inside them, sparks of energy rippling away from a glowing blue core.

The creatures floated above the rough terrain, kicking up tiny clouds of dust everywhere their energy tendrils touched. They appeared to glance around, or at least that was the impression Asya got from their movements.

It wasn't like she could tell what they were doing.

She was just glad to be cloaked and out of sight.

Then one of the aliens turned in what she believed was their direction, and she had the strange feeling that it had seen them.

"Fuck," she growled. "Run!"

"Why?" Ka'nak asked. "It's not like they—"

A glowing bolt of bluish lightning streaked across the intervening space and slammed into Ka'nak.

He shrieked and flew backward, crashing against the rocky wall behind him, kicking up a storm or reddish dust.

His eyes were wide behind the visor. He groaned, trying to focus and clear his head.

Asya ducked another of the bolts and raced to his side, scooping him up and dragging him to his feet.

"We are so fucked," he muttered.

Asya couldn't agree more.

The pair of them hobbled off, but she could hear the creatures coming after them. The ground crackled at their passage, and they were coming fast—much faster than she could move dragging the stunned Melowi.

She looked for a place to hide but realized it was useless. Despite the blow to Ka'nak, he was still cloaked, as was she, yet the aliens had known exactly where they were.

Finding a rock to cower behind wasn't going to help any.

Neither was running.

"We have to fight," she told the warrior.

He nodded and pulled away from her, but he still wobbled on his feet.

There was nothing she could do for him, so she pulled out her weapons and eased down behind a small boulder while he struggled to do the same.

She triggered her comm and reached out to Geroux.

"Looks like we're not going to make it," she told the young tech, sending along the video of what her visor was currently seeing. "Whatever these creatures are, they can see past our cloaks."

"I'm on my way," Geroux shouted, desperation in her voice.

"No," Asya screamed back. The last thing she wanted was for Geroux to suffer the same fate as her and Ka'nak. "Stay with Aht Gow, and stay the hell out of sight. You need to warn Reynolds and the others when they return."

"But I can—" Geroux started, but Asya cut her off as the alien floated over the rock she was hiding behind.

"No, you can't do shit for us. Stay put! That's an order," Asya snarled as she backed away, raising her weapon.

Another of the aliens went at Ka'nak as he lashed out at it. There was a brilliant flash, and the Melowi warrior stumbled and fell face-first to the ground, his weapon jarred from his hands. It hit the dirt.

Asya pulled the trigger, the sound of her weapon drowning out whatever Geroux had shouted over the comm.

Her blast slammed into the alien, distorting its gelatinous body and twisting it sideways. And for the briefest of instants, Asya believed she had a chance.

Then the creature shrugged off the blast and ejected streams of blue lightning to engulf her.

She felt a sharp, agonizing pain as her nerves were short-circuited. She dropped into a heap, unable to control her body.

Fortunately, the pain only lasted a moment.

Then the darkness came and swept her away.

Geroux stifled a gasp as she heard Asya cry out, and her stomach churned as the images of her last few seconds played across her visor. Geroux stumbled, nearly toppling over, thinking Asya and Ka'nak dead.

And then she spotted the strange alien leaning over the visor and appearing to look inside.

Geroux realized that the suit was still relaying what was

going on. Asya's view jumped and twitched, and then rose into the air. The creature had picked the captain up, and she heard her moan at the motion.

She was still alive.

Asya was swung about, and Geroux caught a fleeting glimpse of Ka'nak. The Melowi struggled weakly in the grasp of his captor, although that was *all* she could make out as the screen shorted and went black.

Geroux knew then that they had been captured, and her worry and fear metamorphosed into raging fury and the need to go after her friends.

She glanced down the street at the still-retreating Aht Gow. The aliens' arrival had something to do with the signal the female had sent.

Of that, she had no doubt.

As she stared after the emperor's sister, an idea came to mind.

If she wanted to rescue her friends, she knew what she needed to do.

CHAPTER TEN

The SD *Reynolds* drifted in space, directionless.

Reynolds stood near Tactical's post, staring at the viewscreen, parsing the data as it scrolled. Jiya had run off to oversee the care of the wounded in the med-bay, and Reynolds had stayed at his post to direct the repairs of the ship and coordinate from there.

The bots were working tirelessly to patch the holes in the hull alongside a number of the crew, and XO scrambled to get the gravitic shields back to operational. He'd managed to pull some power from non-essential systems and get them back up, but they were currently running at twelve percent—enough to keep asteroid chunks from hitting, but not enough to stop a determined enemy.

The weapon systems were still operational, but it had taken the ESD to destroy the alien superdreadnought. There was no way they could trigger the weapon now without blowing out all their systems and leaving them even more helpless than they already were.

Outside of the Loranian ship, which had survived the

weapon due to a systems error, he had never seen another ship take the ESD without being obliterated. That this alien craft had not been completely destroyed concerned him.

He'd unloaded his greatest weapon on the enemy and was only able to kill one of them. And now two more were hunting him. The odds weren't good.

"Sitrep," he requested.

Various locations across the ship replied, updating him on the status of their operations. While the ship was badly damaged, it was still serviceable. It would take some time to repair it and return the SD *Reynolds* to its former glory, but it would survive.

The same couldn't be said for a number of the crew.

At last report, thirty-two of his people had died, and several more lives hung in the balance, dependent on how quickly everyone could be stabilized and moved out of the Pod-docs to make room for others.

The whole process was taking too much time, and Reynolds worried they'd lose more.

He'd redirected a number of the bots to the med-bay, as well as several of his split personalities, in order to help where they could. Any extra hands—or brains—he could provide would make things easier for everyone involved.

He still didn't have a clue as to who the aliens who had attacked them were. Reynolds had scoured the databases for ships that were close to matching the description of the one they'd faced, but he'd found nothing.

It was as if the beings didn't exist before today, and their technology was far more powerful than the *Reynolds'*.

More powerful than anything in the universe, even the Kurtherians, and that scared the AI.

He slammed a fist on the console. "Damn it! There has to be something."

Proximity alarms sounded then, and Reynolds spun, wide-eyed.

Ria bolted upright in her seat. "A Gate's opening ahead of us," she announced, her voice trembling.

"Adjust shields," Reynolds ordered. "Fire at the first opportunity, Tactical."

"Another gate is opening to our stern," Ria reported. "It's the enemy superdreadnoughts."

The words sank into Reynolds' ears and made his AI brain churn inside his android skull.

Caught between two of the ships, which had proven to be both more powerful and quicker, there was nowhere to go.

Even if he could open a Gate in time, the ships would destroy them before they slipped through.

"Fucking hell," he muttered. "I hate these guys."

Reynolds straightened and glared at the alien ship hovering on the screen in front of him.

"You ever get a chance to send that 'fuck you' message to the ship we blasted, Comm?" he asked.

"Think now's a good time?" Comm asked back.

"Might be the only way we go out on our own terms," Reynolds said, hating to admit it. "Give me the comm. I want to send this shit myself."

"Might want to hold off on that," Comm told him. "We're being hailed."

Reynolds stiffened at hearing that. Although he understood what Comm had said, for some reason it didn't seem to make sense to him.

"What?"

"The alien ships are hailing us," Comm repeated.

"Put it on the screen," the captain finally ordered.

A moment later, an image of a strange alien appeared, and Reynolds heard Maddox gasp behind him.

On the screen was a blob of pulsing energy that floated in the air like a gooey storm cloud engulfed in blue lightning.

It had no face, although Reynolds could tell the thing was looking at him, even if he wasn't sure how.

A high-pitched whine came through the screen, reminding Reynolds of the recording he'd heard of the first computer modems on Earth.

It was harsh and discordant, and Reynolds couldn't make out a damn bit of it.

"Is that the sound you heard before they attacked?" he whispered to Comm over his shoulder. "It sounds like the 90s. Do these pricks work for AOL?"

"It sounds similar," Comm confirmed.

Reynolds turned back to the creature and raised his hands in a gesture he hoped conveyed that he had no fucking clue what the thing was trying to say.

"Trying to clean it up, but I'm not having much success," Comm told him.

The creature seemed to understand that the crew were struggling to understand it, and it drifted sideways and motioned as if it were looking behind itself. Then the creature turned back, and a strong, clear voice rang out across the speakers.

"I am Xyxl, captain of the Gulg superdreadnought *Qqhrt*," the alien said, or actually some automated voice the creature was using. "Mimicking approximate language, so forgive errors in communicate."

Reynolds sighed in relief, even though he wanted to tear into the aliens for attacking them, but he knew now wasn't the time to stand on principle and put all their lives at risk.

He'd return their faux-politeness as best he could and wait for the right opportunity to pay them back for the souls they'd taken.

He took a moment to muster his restraint and nodded to the creature, introducing himself.

"I am Reynolds, captain of the Federation superdread-nought *Reynolds*." Reynolds kept it short without threat or explanation.

The creature went on as if Reynolds hadn't spoken.

"You provide access to databases immediately," the creature demanded.

Reynolds scoffed. "That's not going to happen, phlegm-boy." The words were out before he could rein them in.

He wasn't used to dealing with beings who could destroy him.

The aliens didn't appear offended.

"Open databases to review," it repeated.

"I can't allow you access to my information, regardless of how powerful or entitled you think you are," Reynolds responded. "I will scuttle the ship before I let you scrape my databases or hurt my crew again."

The alien floated on the screen a moment without

saying anything, appearing to contemplate the ultimatum Reynolds had given it.

"You *must* open databases," the alien pressed. "We cannot proceed. Imperative."

Reynolds snarled and shook his head.

"What we're having here is a failure to communicate," Tactical growled. "What part of 'Fuck off and die horribly' do you not understand?"

Flickers of energy ran through the alien's form, making it appear agitated, but the calm, smooth voice that rang out over the speakers betrayed none of its apparent frustration.

"You *will* open your databases," it said.

"That was pretty clear," Comm whispered.

Reynolds cut the sound on the channel and glanced over his shoulder at Comm. "Which one of these fucking ships is this asshole on?"

Comm examined the signal, and Reynolds could sense the uncertainty in his split personality's pause.

"Uh…neither?"

"What do you mean?" Reynolds snarled. "How can he be speaking to us if he's not on one of them?"

"The signal is coming from the Quadrain system," Comm told him. "Ostensibly this guy is still on the planet."

"How is that possible?" Reynolds asked.

"Fuck if I know," Comm responded, "but that's where I'm tracing it to, although they're trying to obscure it. It's the same shit Jora'nal pulled on Gorad's ships…only different."

"Way to clarify," Tactical told him.

"There's a similarity in the coding, but it's not the same," Comm went on.

Reynolds turned around and looked back at the screen, splitting his focus between the strange creature and the nearby console that scrolled with intel. He tapped a few keys on the console, expanding the SD *Reynolds'* scanner range.

What he saw made his AI mind whirl.

He turned back to the alien and unmuted the channel.

"How is it you can speak to us from so far away?" he asked.

"Expose databases," the creature repeated.

Reynolds snarled.

"I'll open a single file to you before we go further, but nothing else," Reynolds told the creature, glancing back at Comm's station. "Give them access to our translator data. I'm tired of talking to a petulant five-year-old."

Comm opened access to the file, acknowledging that they'd collected it from the system right away, and Reynolds watched as the alien seemed to process it. A second later, another demand came over the comm.

"We must examine your databases to assure that you are not a threat to us," the creature said, speaking more clearly this time "You have destroyed one of our ships, and we must understand your systems before we determine your fate."

"Oh, yeah, that's better." Tactical groaned. "These guys want to be the judge, jury, and assacutioner all in one."

"Yeah, you're worried we're a threat to you, huh?" Reynolds grumbled.

Then he thought about it for a moment.

Maybe we are.

Given that the enemy wanted their databases so badly,

it was clear that they didn't understand the type of weapon that had been used on them. They didn't know how much energy it took for the superdreadnought to activate it, and they didn't know how much it took out of the *Reynolds* to fire it.

They could use that to their advantage, Reynolds realized.

But before he could think of how, alarms flashed across the bridge.

"Uh oh, it looks like we have a problem," Comm mumbled. "They're riding in on that file transmission and trying to hack into the system."

"Well, fucking stop them," Reynolds demanded.

"Easier said than done," Comm complained.

"What do you mean?" Reynolds asked.

"These guys are good," Comm replied. "*Reeeeal* good."

"Then you better damn well bring your A-game, Comm," Reynolds snarled. "If these motherfuckers get into the system, we're screwed. Keep them out."

"Working on it," Comm mumbled, uncertainty in his computer voice. "They're coming at us in that weird-ass language of theirs, and it's obfuscating some of their efforts. This shit is strange."

"Well, *unweird* it, damn it," Reynolds growled.

The power flickered on the bridge as an unseen battle was waged.

"It's a good thing we bumped up our security since the Gorad confrontation," Maddox said. Sweat beaded his forehead. "They're hitting the system hard. My console is glitching."

"Keep on knocking, but you can't come in," Tactical sang.

"That might not be the case, Tactical. They're cracking through and scraping the surface of our databases," Comm complained, sounding desperate. "I can't keep them out of the rest of the systems for long. These guys are just too good."

And that was when it clicked.

"The fog of my mind has cleared!" Reynolds realized something he should have known earlier.

He triggered the comm, his voice echoing throughout the ship. "All of me, I need you to fucking pay attention," he called. "We have an intruder trying to hack our systems. I need each and every one of you to dial in and work together to repel them, and I need you to do it right fucking now!"

Reynolds jumped on his console and got to work. He knew immediately that his other personalities had joined him as he reconnected his higher processes in the harrowing fight to hold off the strange aliens.

Comm sighed. "That's working."

Reynolds growled in reply, "We've been working below our normal operational level with the split," he explained. "It doesn't affect our general function when it comes to day-to-day tasks, but by doing everything individually, it's like we're doing things with some of our senses muffled."

"I *thought* you had your head up your ass," Tactical told him.

"And it smelled like you," Reynolds fired back. "Organize the process as if we're a single unit because, well, we *are*, assholes."

And they did.

With all the computing power of the AI personalities focused on a single task, the alien hacker soon retreated, its efforts to crack *Reynolds'* databases repelled.

"We're locking them out," Comm announced, relief in his voice. "They're back behind the firewall now. Additional security protocols are in place to keep them there."

"Take that, squealy," Tactical shouted.

The alien on the screen looked at something behind it, then turned back to Reynolds.

"You have repelled us from your systems," it said, a hint of surprise coming through even the automated computer voice it used.

"Damn straight we did," Tactical told the alien.

"Since we are unable to confirm what is necessary, prepare to be boarded," Xyxl stated.

"I don't fucking think so," Reynolds snarled. "Any ship you send our direction will be blasted to dust," the AI warned. "Keep your distance."

The viewscreen went black as the connection was severed.

"Chattus interruptus is so disappointing," Tactical said.

"You don't think they'll actually try to board us, do you?" Maddox asked.

Reynolds shrugged. "I don't think so, but it's not like they can line their superdreadnoughts up beside us to do it," he answered. "That means they have to use smaller, more vulnerable craft to accomplish it. Craft we can blow the fuck out of. Ready weapons, Tactical."

"Ready and waiting," Tactical replied. "Anyone who gets

near us is going to eat a big-ass heaping mouthful of scorching death."

"Greetings, Federation," a strange voice said, the sound coming across the SD *Reynolds'* speaker system. A flicker of energy sounded at their backs.

Everyone on the bridge spun about and stared.

"Uh…sir?" Ria mumbled, her trembling hand in the air, pointing. "We've got company." Her voice wavered.

Three of the aliens floated in the open area in front of the large viewscreen on the bridge.

"What the fuck?" Maddox cursed, eyes wide. "How did…"

The general went for his gun, but Reynolds held up a hand to stop him when he saw the energy forms of the creatures. Maddox reluctantly resisted the urge to defy the order.

There was a piercing *squee* through the speakers, then the alien's voice seemed to resonate from the being, Reynolds translator systems parsing what was being said directly.

"Be aware that we mean you no harm," the alien Reynolds assumed was Xyxl said.

"Except, you *did* cause harm," he fired back. "A number of our crew are dead, thanks to you and your actions."

"We assessed you as a threat when you arrived so suddenly and acted accordingly," Xyxl replied, his voice even more casual directly, although it carried a staticky undertone that grated on Reynolds' ears.

"How about we blow your alien asses off our bridge?" Tactical shouted.

Reynolds felt a wave of pressure wash over him as if the aliens were examining him. Then the feeling disappeared.

"Your weapons are incapable of harming us," Xyxl stated matter-of-factly, confirming what Reynolds had already determined. The alien drifted closer to the captain without apparent fear, leaving its two companions behind. "I extend our apologies for your losses. Our scans defined you as an enemy."

"And your firing on us defined *you* as an enemy of *ours*," Reynolds said coldly.

The alien drifted even closer, and Reynolds felt the wave of energy pass over him again.

They're scanning me.

"You appear human, yet you are not," Xyxl mused. "You are a construct."

"What do you know about humans?" Reynolds asked, ignoring the part about him being an android.

The alien appeared to stare at Reynolds for a quiet moment before finally speaking. "We know much about you, of your Federation and Queen, about your mission," Xyxl answered. "It required us to examine your databases to be sure, however."

"You didn't get shit, though," Tactical sniped. "You know nothing."

"On the contrary, we learned all we needed before you managed to lock us out," Xyxl countered. "That is why we determined it would be best for us to conduct our discussions face to face."

"So, what do you have to say?" Reynolds asked, holding his position against the ball of energy.

"We apologize, and have come to repair the damage we have caused."

"We appreciate the assistance, but you won't have access to our systems for anything you'll do," Reynolds stated. "And what makes you think we want anything from you?"

"Because we can bring your crew back from the brink if you allow us to," the alien told him.

"Wait, you can bring them back to life?" Maddox asked to clarify.

"Indeed," Xyxl answered. "If done soon enough. Time is of the essence, however. It must be done quickly."

Reynolds stiffened. He hadn't expected *that*. Now he was stuck in a situation where he had to decide whether to play nice with the weird aliens in the hopes that they could actually bring his people back to life, or reject them and accept the consequences of having lost crew.

Time was running out. He had to decide, but one question nagged him, caused him to hesitate.

"This enemy you believed us to be," Reynolds asked. "Who are they?"

"Why, the Kurtherians, of course."

CHAPTER ELEVEN

Geroux followed the emperor's sister through Ulf, her thoughts whirling.

Never before had she contemplated doing what she imagined, but she'd never been in such a situation before.

Her stomach was a clenched knot of anticipation and rage and uncertainty, but she was committed. Geroux had to do something to ensure that Asya and Ka'nak were safe, and there was only one thing she could think of to make that happen.

Geroux eased closer to Aht Gow as she strode on, oblivious that Geroux was following her. She did her best to avoid contact with passersby.

Aht Gow twisted and turned and wound her way through the city, each successive direction change moving her farther from the busy streets into the quiet, nearly abandoned alleyways that ran behind the buildings and homes.

Geroux had a moment of doubt as she pictured the emperor's sister leading her into a trap, but she extended the scanners of her suit and confirmed that she was alone with the Muultu. The alley they were in, and those nearby, were empty of people.

If she was going to do what she planned, it needed to be now.

Geroux swallowed hard and darted forward, doing her best to muffle the sound of her approach. Breath held in check, lungs throbbing, she closed the distance.

Even then she wondered if she could do what was necessary, but a cold, rational voice inside her pushed her on.

It was this or risk her friends being killed.

She couldn't let that happen.

Geroux came up behind Aht Gow before the emperor's sister realized she was there.

A scuff of a boot at the last second alerted Aht Gow and she spun, eyes wide, although Geroux knew she couldn't see anything thanks to the armor's cloaking. She raised her hands out of instinct at the same time Geroux closed, but there was nothing the female could do to stop her.

The young tech's hand clenched into a fist and shot forward. Aht Gow opened her mouth to shriek, but before she could make a sound, Geroux punched her hard in the forehead.

There was a solid *thump* as reinforced knuckles collided with bone and Aht Gow stumbled backward, eyes spinning in their sockets. She gasped and fell to a knee.

Geroux growled when the Muultu reeled, a flash of conflicting emotions running through her at seeing her still awake, but she hadn't started this to quit now.

She pulled back her hand and hit the emperor's sister again, driving her to the ground.

Aht Gow lay there stiffly, unconscious.

Geroux sighed, staring down at the female, unsure how to feel about what she'd just done to her.

But there wasn't time for that. Asya and Ka'nak needed her.

She scooped up Aht Gow and tossed her over her shoulder, checking her system to ensure that the armor's cloaking device extended to the alien's limp body. Once Geroux was sure that both she and the emperor's sister were obscured, she started off again.

With her hostage, Geroux made her way to where Asya and Ka'nak had last been seen.

That was as far ahead as she'd planned.

Fortunately, it would be a while before she reached them.

She'd have plenty of time to think of something by then.

At least she hoped she would.

Asya blinked and came awake with a start, through blurred vision and disorientation she struggled to collect her wits.

She gasped and tried to fling herself upward, only to feel a weight push her back to the hard floor. Asya growled in defiance, glancing over when she heard Ka'nak mumble something.

"Relax, or you'll hurt yourself," he told her, his gravelly

voice indicating he was barely more awake than she was. He was propped in a stone pew to the side of her.

She twisted her head to glance at the Melowi and saw that he was being held in place by some kind of forcefield. It was wrapped about him in strips like rope and glistened with his every subtle movement.

Asya realized she, too, was held in place by the same kind of field. The straps tightened every time she tried to shift or adjust, growing uncomfortable for a moment before relaxing once she stopped fighting them.

They were in what appeared to be the ruins of an old church. It struck her then that they hadn't been moved far.

"They brought us inside?" she asked.

"Looks that way," Ka'nak answered. "Our hosts are right over there." He gestured toward the front of the church with his chin.

Asya stared across the intervening space and spotted the two strange aliens who had captured them. They floated alongside the main cultist, who stood on a small dais at the front of the room. He was pointing at Asya and Ka'nak.

Where his people had gone, she didn't know. They were nowhere to be seen.

The aliens and the cult leader came over to stand—float—in front of Asya and Ka'nak.

A sharp, ear-piercing *skree* sounded before the alien's voice became something she could understand.

"Who are you?" the alien asked.

"We're the people who are going to bring down you and your bullshit cult," she snarled. "We know all about

Phraim-'Eh and his people and their connections, and that asshole Jora'nal in the Loranian ship," she went on.

While she really didn't have much in the way of details, Asya figured it couldn't hurt to bluster. The aliens had captured them instead of killing them. That meant they wanted something.

Most likely, it was to interrogate her and the Melowi to see what they knew, and what could be used against the *Reynolds* and its crew.

Asya wouldn't let that happen.

She'd stir the pot and see what she could find out about their enemy first while trying to turn the table.

"Our superdreadnought is in orbit, and they know exactly where we are," she continued. "If you think they're going to leave us here alone and at your mercy, you're sadly mistaken. They're positioning themselves right now to blow the shit out of you."

The cultist growled and turned on the nearest alien. "This was a mistake," he said. "The longer we entertain these beings here on Muultar, the greater the risk that we expose ourselves to the others."

"You're not going to be exposed," Asya fired back. "You're going to be exterminated."

The cultist spun away. "We are wasting our time. Be rid of them." He marched toward the front of the church, fuming, his every step heavy and angry.

The aliens appeared unaffected by his tirade.

"If you want to be rid of us," Ka'nak started, "you can simply let us go. We can pretend none of this ever happened. We can keep our mouths shut."

The aliens peered at them, their internal energies flickering as if in contemplation.

"I can sense your concern," one of the aliens said, "but I believe it is due to your uncertainty regarding us and our mission here."

"Give that freaky alien a prize," Asya muttered. "You think?"

The alien seemed to sigh. "Things are not as they might appear," he stated. "Perhaps I should show you."

"Yeah, why don't you do that," Asya growled.

A tendril of energy fluttered and the restraining bands fell away, freeing Ka'nak and Asya. The pair scrambled to their feet.

Asya hadn't expected it to be that easy.

"Come with me and I will," the alien said, drifting toward the front of the church where the cultist sulked. The other followed.

Ka'nak glanced at her and shrugged.

"What the hell?" she said and started off after the glowing energy, deciding against trying to flee. "What have we got to lose?"

"Everything?" Ka'nak countered.

"Well, yeah, there is that."

But if the aliens had wanted to kill them, they would have done it by now. They had something else in mind, and Asya wanted to know what that was.

"You thought we were Kurtherians?" Reynolds asked,

shocked to hear what the alien had said and still uncertain if he'd really heard it.

"Your energy signatures, while markedly different, contain an aspect of Kurtherian technology," Xyxl told him.

"As do yours," Tactical fired back.

The alien almost seemed to nod. "This is true," he replied. "Like you and your people, we have been influenced in some small manner by our enemies. We have adopted what technology we could, and have adapted it to our own uses. This, as we have both seen, only sows confusion."

"Yeah, like random aliens blasting us for no reason," Tactical growled. "Killing our meatbags for no reason."

Reynolds waved his other personality to silence. "Speaking of our people," he started, "you claim to be able to bring our dead back to life?"

"That is technically incorrect," Xyxl clarified, "but we can help them, yes."

"How?" Reynolds questioned, feeling the press of time on his shoulders.

"Like all living beings, your crew is made up of electrical impulses that control their every action and their very existence. And although you understand much of their physiology, there is a deeper mechanism that avoids you. This stage precedes *true* death."

"There were a lot of words there, but you're not saying much," Tactical muttered.

"My point is, while you believe your crew to be dead, their electrical impulses below the threshold of detectable activity to your science, your people are not yet effectively dead. We can restart them."

"How about we skip the details for now and just do it?" Reynolds pressed. "You mentioned us being short on time, remember?"

"Of course," Xyxl replied.

The alien seemed to pulse, flickers of current growing in its center as if a lightning storm rippled through a cloud, and then there was a wash of energy that flared out, running over all of them and deeper into the ship.

Reynolds gasped as his circuits flashed and felt as if they were on fire for an instant, then the feeling passed.

He glanced around the bridge and saw Maddox and Ria rubbing their temples as if they'd had a sudden headache come on, but neither looked seriously harmed, just in discomfort.

"It is done," Xyxl stated.

"That's it?" Tactical asked, obvious distrust in his tone of voice. "You just send out a sparkly blast of energy and everything's okay?"

The comm activated then, and Jiya's shaky voice came through. "Uh…you know all those dead people we lined up in the hallway outside of the med-bay? Well, they just…uh, sat up."

Reynolds activated the ship's cameras and zoomed in on the hall where Jiya and the others had placed their dead crewmates in anticipation of their eventual funeral rites and burial in space.

His crew sat up, shocked, eyes wide, and then the panic and pain set in.

People screamed and howled and fell back, clasping at their wounds. Blood began to flow.

"Oh, fuck!" Jiya screamed over the comm. "They're still hurt."

She was only baffled for an instant before regaining her composure and ordering the once dead but now wounded into the Pod-docs for stabilization.

She didn't bother to say anything to Reynolds, simply cut the connection and got to work saving her crew.

Reynolds ordered the bots and the rest of the available crew to help her, and he spun on the alien with a growl.

"How come you didn't warn us that they would come back with all their injuries intact?" the AI shouted.

The alien seemed to shrug, his energy tendrils fluttering. "We had not discussed such contingencies," he answered. "We only spoke of returning them to sentience, and didn't believe the rest to be of concern."

"Guess you don't know as much about humans as you claimed," Maddox snarled, shaking his head. He hopped up, headed toward the bridge door. "I'm going to—"

"Jiya has it under control," Reynolds told the general, waving him back to his station.

Maddox grimaced but dropped back into his seat without being told again. Reynolds knew the general was fighting his instincts to go help his crew, but the AI was coordinating with Jiya through the doctor aspect of his personality. He figured Maddox knew that.

They had already prioritized those of the crew who needed the Pod-docs the most and were cycling them into the system, while stabilizing and taking care of those who could wait; those whose injuries wouldn't kill them again now that they had been brought back to life.

Well, if the aliens were to be believed, none of them had

truly been dead, so they hadn't technically been resurrected. They'd been...*restarted?*

It was a concept Reynolds wanted to look into more thoroughly, but now wasn't the time to try to figure it out. They had other issues to discuss.

"We're not engaging on the same level," Reynolds muttered to the alien.

"There is much that we can learn from one another," Xyxl admitted. "Given our common enemy, it would appear it would be in our best interests to commit to a true dialogue between us."

"We're not letting you scrape our databases," Reynolds warned.

Xyxl seemed to laugh, the sound awkward and strange. "We have no need to examine your databases any longer," he said. "We know of your healing technology and the secret of your nanocytes. At least the theory of such," Xyxl finished. "That was not what we were looking for, fear not."

If Reynolds had had a physical heart, it would have skipped a beat at hearing that.

Xyxl went on, "Much of our technology is similar to yours and our evolution proceeded along the same lines, although we have had longer to develop ours," he said. "We can do what you can, and more."

"Which explains how you just appeared on our ship without effort," Tactical grunted.

"Something we might not have been able to do had your gravitic shields been stronger than they are now," Xyxl admitted.

Reynolds filed that detail away for later use.

"Now that we've established that we're on the same side and have a common enemy, there's something else we need to talk about."

"And that is?" Xyxl asked.

"What is your connection to Phraim-'Eh and his cult?" Reynolds replied.

"Ahh," Xyxl said, pausing a moment. "That is complicated, and I believe it might be easier to show you than to explain it."

"How do you plan to do that?" Reynold asked.

"You must come with us," Xyxl answered simply.

Reynolds scoffed. "Maybe you haven't noticed, but now's not exactly a good time for us to be gallivanting about the universe. We've got wounded people to see to, and we're on a mission. We need to talk about your influence on Muultar."

"And we shall, Reynolds," Xyxl told him. "They are all connected."

"Then let's get to talking," Reynolds went on as a pulse of energy washed over him.

He realized he was no longer on the superdreadnought's bridge.

***

Maddox gasped when Reynolds and the aliens disappeared without warning.

One second they were there talking, and the next they were gone, vanished without a trace.

"Where did they go?" the general asked, looking around.

Ensign Alcott slowly shook her head as she stared at the empty space where the captain had been. "They just disappeared. Scanners aren't picking up Reynolds anywhere aboard the ship."

"The two alien superdreadnoughts are pulling back," Comm reported, the individual AI personalities having returned to their posts after the consolidated effort to repel the intruders. "They're headed back to the planet at max speed."

"That answers where they took Reynolds," Tactical growled. "They said they wanted to show him something."

"Where does that leave us?" Maddox asked, scratching at his chin.

"Fucked?" Tactical countered.

"Sounds about right," the general replied. "Follow those superdreadnoughts wherever they go. Get close enough that when they Gate, we can use theirs," he ordered.

"Yes, sir," Ria answered, acting on the order.

The SD *Reynolds* came about and started after the other ships despite its damage.

"You sure this is a good idea?" XO asked. "We're not exactly in fighting shape here. What happens if they turn on us?"

Maddox shrugged. "Then we're likely dead," he answered, "but I don't think that's what these guys want, or they wouldn't have done what they did with the crew. Why bring people back to life just to kill them again?"

"Maybe not," XO replied, "but that doesn't mean we're not vulnerable out here. We could run into someone else, or Reynolds could piss these alien bastards off and they could turn on us."

Tactical groaned. "I'm betting on the latter."

"Then we continue to work on repairs and get our ship in order," the general said, "but I'm not going to leave Reynolds in these guys' hands. He wouldn't do it to us, and we damn sure won't do it to him."

Only silence answered that, and Maddox knew he'd gotten through to the other AI personalities. They might fight and argue and contradict each other, but when it came to loyalty, there was no question.

They would do whatever was required to ensure that Reynolds was okay.

That settled, they just needed to figure out how to go about getting Reynolds back.

One problem at a time, Maddox thought.

CHAPTER TWELVE

After reaching out to San Roche, Geroux arrived near the strange natural church that Asya and Ka'nak had been captured outside of.

The cloaked Pod hovered in the near distance, giving Geroux a tactical view of the surrounding area.

Sadly, there wasn't much to see.

An alien ship was perched outside the stone building that had been carved into the landscape. Scanners told her that it was unoccupied, although its defenses remained up and the ship at the ready.

She scanned further and picked up the energy signatures of Asya and Ka'nak inside the church, as well as three other lifeforms, two of which were so alien as to defy description. They appeared as balls of energy that came back weirdly on the scans, confusing the system as to what kind of creatures they were.

Outside were five of the cultists who had left the estate with the first, the one Geroux assumed was inside the church with Asya and Ka'nak.

"What do you intend to do with me?" Aht Gow asked, a mix of fear and inborn arrogance coming out in her snarl. "I am Emperor Krol Gow's blood sister. He will not tolerate such mistreatment of me."

"I know who you are," Geroux shot back. "And right now I don't give a damn what your brother thinks. You're conspiring with our enemy, and your friends have kidnapped mine. Until I get them back, you're not going anywhere, no matter how much you bitch and complain and try to throw your weight around."

Aht Gow stiffened in the straps that Geroux had used to bind her, her eyes narrow slits as she glared at Geroux.

Geroux turned away from the emperor's sister, wanting nothing to do with the female beyond trading her for her friends.

Unfortunately, Geroux hadn't figured out the best way to do that yet.

She'd watched Asya and Ka'nak being taken down easily by the aliens, and she knew damn well she didn't stand a chance against them in combat if those two had been so easily disarmed. She couldn't bull her way and demand a trade.

No, she had to figure out how to entice the enemy with the emperor's sister while avoiding being captured or killed herself.

"This will not end well for you," Aht Gow told her.

"Want me to gag her?" San Roche asked.

Geroux was tempted. She couldn't think with the Muultu prattling on. But she decided against it.

The more the emperor's sister talked, the more likely it was that she would reveal something she didn't intend to.

Geroux hoped that something would help her figure out how to get her friends back safely.

She also hoped it would come soon.

"My master will strike you down if my brother does not," she threatened. "He will not allow such indignities to go unpunished."

San Roche raised a curious eyebrow at her statement.

"Your master?" Geroux prodded, hoping to get more information.

"Phraim-'Eh will bring his vengeance down upon you," she said. "I know who you are, and my master will reward me greatly for bringing you to him."

Hearing the female implicate herself in the schemes of Phraim-'Eh and his cult so openly made Geroux sick.

That meant that the aliens down there in the church were working for Phraim-'Eh, too. Asya and Ka'nak were in serious trouble.

Geroux swallowed hard at the thought.

She turned away from Aht Gow and stared at the console in front of her. Her fingers danced across the keypad as she widened her scans of the area, looking for something—anything—to steer her in the right direction.

She didn't find a clue, but she did find something else.

Geroux groaned as the scanners picked up the same type of signal emanating from the church as had been streaming from the estate where she found Aht Gow.

"Damn it," she muttered.

Distracted by the thought of confronting the enemy who'd captured Asya and Ka'nak, Geroux hadn't thought to look for a signal beamed into space. She'd believed the one Aht Gow had sent to be a one-time thing, her reaching out to her contacts, these strange aliens; she hadn't expected to find the same thing here.

But there it was.

She leaned closer to the screen to examine the data flowing across it and, while she couldn't interpret the information being sent spaceward, it was clear it was some kind of communication beam, just like the other beam had been.

This one, however, didn't have the same urgency as the other. It seemed more stationary, continuous rather than the short burst of the message Aht Gow had sent to her people.

It also appeared to be emanating from the mountain as opposed to the church. Or rather, from *within* the mountain, but there was some sort of interference that kept her from pinpointing its source exactly.

"What is this place?" she asked Aht Gow.

"It is the temple to our god, Phraim-'Eh," she snarled. "A sacred place of worship, where those of us who believe mingle with others of similar bent."

"Bent?" Geroux asked. "More like twisted and snapped."

"Make fun as you will, heathen, but Phraim-'Eh will have his revenge, and you will regret such heresy."

"I regret a lot of things," Geroux told her. "The first of which is not letting San Roche here gag you."

"Jora'nal and the Voice of Phraim-'Eh will hunt you down and teach you the error of your ways," Aht Gow threatened. "My lord will know of what you have done, and they will come for you."

Geroux had heard enough.

She hopped up and went over to the emperor's sister,

tearing a strip from the female's shawl. Then she wound the piece up and wrapped it around her head, effectively gagging Aht Gow.

The emperor's sister chewed and gnawed at the makeshift gag, trying to dislodge it, but it kept her complaints to a minimum.

She went on growling and threatening, but Geroux couldn't make out what she was saying, and that was good enough.

"What are we going to do?" San Roche asked.

Geroux still wasn't sure. She thought to blast the alien ship, but given the readings from the scanners, she couldn't be sure that the Pod had the power to take it out before it returned fire.

She didn't know if the Pod could withstand an attack either, since opening fire would reveal their location to the enemy.

She also couldn't be sure that the aliens wouldn't hurt Asya and Ka'nak in response to whatever she did.

Geroux stared at the church, letting her mind run through the problem in search of a conclusion that didn't put them all at risk.

She didn't have time to find one before the enemy forced her hand.

"Someone's coming out of the church," San Roche reported, pointing at the viewscreen.

Geroux hissed and followed his finger.

Asya and Ka'nak marched out of the stone building. Behind them, the cultist stomped and the aliens floated, all of them joining the group of five who had lingered outside.

"That's a lot of bad guys," Geroux muttered under her breath.

As badly as she didn't want to face off with eight of the enemy, they had forced her hand by leaving the church. The group was headed toward the alien ship, and if they reached it, there would be nothing Geroux could do to rescue her friends.

"Damn it," she growled, grabbing the emperor's sister and hauling her to her feet.

The Muultu snarled and frothed, but Geroux couldn't understand a word.

"Drop me off here, then get back into the air to provide cover," Geroux ordered. "I want you to be ready to shoot these guys down. Whatever happens, don't let them get into that ship, understand?"

San Roche grunted. "I'll do my best," he said as he dropped the Pod behind a nearby rise and let Geroux and her prisoner out, unseen by the enemy.

Not more than a few seconds later, the hatch closed and the cloaked Pod disappeared from view again. A waft of air washed over her, and Geroux started off around the hill, knowing that San Roche had moved the Pod into place as she'd ordered.

Geroux drew a deep breath and triggered her personal cloaking device, extending it to envelop Aht Gow.

Effectively invisible now, Geroux hurried around the rise, dragging the emperor's sister along with her. Although she hadn't wanted to, she felt it best to give the appearance of being threatening, so she pulled her pistol out and pressed it to the female's side.

It wasn't much of a threat while she was cloaked, but

she wanted to get used to the idea of holding a hostage at gunpoint. She needed to look comfortable once she uncloaked if she was going to pressure the cultists and their alien allies into complying.

As she stepped into the path of the enemy and her captive friends, she contemplated remaining cloaked and risking an attack on them, hoping the element of surprise would overcome the deficit in her fighting ability.

She never got the chance to try.

The aliens stopped abruptly when she arrived.

"There is another here," the first of the alien energy forms stated, an electrical tendril twitching in her direction.

There was a sudden wash of energy, and Geroux's system reported that her cloak had failed.

She cursed when she realized she was now visible to everyone. Aht Gow took in a breath of the harsh, unfiltered air of Muultar and started to cough.

The cultists raised their weapons and pointed them at her, the yawning mouths of their barrels staring her down.

She swallowed hard and let out a threatening growl as she jabbed the gun into Aht Gow's ribs harder. "Lower your weapons or the emperor's sister gets it."

Asya's eyes went wide at seeing her, and the captain gave her a 'what the hell" look. Geroux shrugged. She went to activate the mental link to explain, but Asya rushed forward and stood between her and the cultists and alien.

"Don't shoot, Geroux," Asya told her, pulling the emperor's sister out of her hands before anything could happen to her. "This isn't what it looks like."

Geroux sighed as the cultists lowered their weapons and came to stand around her, the aliens hovering.

"No shit?"

"No shit," Asya assured.

"That's good," Geroux told her. "I didn't have anything planned after this part anyway."

Reynolds no longer stood upon the bridge of the *Reynolds*. The acrid stink of smoke and burnt electronics assailed his nose, and he glanced about to take stock of his situation.

I can't be aboard their superdreadnought since we killed that one, he thought, confusion gripping him. *And it's on the other side of the system.*

That in and of itself was amazing.

The aliens had transported them directly to this ship in the blink of an eye.

Reynolds hadn't figured out their method of interacting with the world yet, but it was clear they operated on a level above any other species he had ever encountered.

That sent a metaphorical chill down his android spine.

"How do you do that?" he asked.

If he could get his hands on the technology to transport himself and the crew through space with a thought, there would be so much he could accomplish in his mission.

The ability to bring the dead back to life would be a nice trick, too.

"As you have your secrets, so do we," Xyxl stated, and though Reynolds couldn't see it, he was sure the alien was smiling.

Reynolds sighed and glanced around the ship, hoping to learn all he could about the alien creatures and their technology. "I thought we destroyed this ship."

"That superdreadnought, alas, was destroyed. This one was behind it at some distance, unobserved by your sensors. It weathered some damage thanks to the cone of destruction from whatever you call that weapon of yours. We've never seen its equal."

"We call it, 'Eat Shit and Die,' or ESD for short." Saying it out loud in calm company made it sound less profound.

"Quaint, but one cannot argue its effectiveness," the alien allowed.

Dozens more of the creatures roamed the bridge, seemingly without direction. Nothing made sense aboard the craft. Where Reynolds would normally see controls and the various stations that made up most starships, there were no identifiable instruments or controls.

Everything was…*alien*.

"You call yourselves Gulg?" Reynolds asked, tired of thinking of the creatures as "aliens."

"The closest translation of our name in your language would be 'the Gulg,'" Xyxl answered.

"And in your language?"

Xyxl emitted a grating, high-pitch shriek that hurt even his android ears before his systems adjusted to the aural assault that went on for several long seconds.

The Gulg seemed to shrug once it was done. "We find it easier to simply let the translation devices of those species we cross fill in a substitute for our name since it often doesn't translate well."

"I'm noticing," Reynolds complained, shaking his head to make the lingering noise go away.

He stopped as soon as he realized he was doing it.

Too much time spent around the crew, he thought. *I'm starting to take on their damn twitchy habits.*

Xyxl stared at Reynolds for a moment, then his energies shifted and he took on the general form of a humanoid, similar in appearance to Reynolds' android body. The alien had a face and features Reynolds could now identify, although the flesh of the Gulg was still transparent, its electrical impulses storming through its differently shaped body much the same as it had the other shape.

"That's…interesting," Reynolds muttered.

"We also find it easier to mimic the form of the species we are relating to in order to make ourselves more familiar," Xyxl said. "Does it help?"

"It's disconcerting, to be honest," Reynolds answered, "but whatever works for you. Humans are what I know best, but I'm not programmed to be negatively impacted by any difference in appearance."

Xyxl nodded, and although Reynolds appreciated the familiar response, he knew better than to let himself be lulled into a more accepting state by it.

No matter what the Gulg looked like, they were still alien, and could easily be attempting to manipulate him with their familiarity.

"So, can I ask why you brought me here?" Reynolds asked, deciding it was best to get down to business. "My crew will be wondering where I am."

"Our ships will lead them here," Xyxl told him. "Until then, we believed it optimal that we speak with you alone since you were the sole representative of the human Federation."

"My crew can be trusted," he answered.

"Perhaps, but it is our understanding that human commanders prefer to be given their intelligence privately, allowing them to disburse it as necessary among their crew."

"That's true," Reynolds replied, "but humans also find it to be an act of war to kidnap their superiors and transport them across the system into strange spacecraft."

The Gulg paused as if he hadn't thought of that.

"As I said earlier, there is much we have to learn about one another," Xyxl said, chuckling.

"Well, how about we get down to it, then?" Reynolds pressed.

He had a feeling the crew would be worried about him, and he was afraid they'd do something stupid in an effort to get him back before things could be explained when they arrived.

"You said you thought we were Kurtherians when you attacked us," Reynolds went on. "Why was that?"

"Well, not Kurtherians per se, but more their descendants," Xyxl said.

"I'm not sure I understand," Reynolds admitted.

"My people have been at war with the Kurtherians for several millennia, but we long ago chased them from our space," the Gulg explained. "Or so we believed. As it turned out, we only succeeded in scattering them across the universe, causing them to dig in elsewhere to continue their expansion."

"So, we have you to blame for them stumbling across Earth?" Reynolds snarled.

The alien shook its head. "No, that was not our doing. They happened upon you on their own. It had nothing to do with our efforts, although I don't imagine that's satisfying to know."

Reynolds agreed that it wasn't.

"So, these *descendants*?" He let the question hang, unsure what he was even asking.

"Those are the beings you encountered upon Muultar," Xyxl went on.

"You're saying Phraim-'Eh and the others, the cultists, are not true Kurtherians?" Reynolds asked.

The alien shook its head. "No, they are not directly descended from the Kurtherians, but more that they have adopted their philosophy and attitudes, taking over where the Kurtherians left off and spreading their chaos across this galaxy."

Reynolds didn't know how to feel about that.

His mission had been to track and kill Kurtherians, and now he was being told that the assholes he'd believed to be Kurtherians really weren't, yet they kind of were.

"Phraim-'Eh and his people can be considered the next generation of the Kurtherian threat," Xyxl told him as if he'd been reading his mind. "They have been equipped by the Kurtherians and made to believe in their mission, so they are just as much the enemy of humanity as the Kurtherians who came before."

"Well, that makes me feel better. Sort of," Reynolds said. "What do you know of Phraim-'Eh?"

"He is a self-styled god who uses his powers to wage

war across the universe," the Gulg answered. "As one of the few of the new generation who have actually had contact with the Kurtherians, he believes it is his mission to wipe out and destroy those who choose the side of the Federation."

"That explains his hard-on for me then," Reynolds grumbled.

"I don't understand your colloquialism, but I believe I understand the intent behind it," Xyxl said. "We, too, have a hard-on for Phraim-'Eh."

Reynolds chuckled. "Probably best that you never say that again, just for future reference," he told the alien. "But if I understand you correctly, you're here to take out Phraim-'Eh and his people, too?"

"We are," Xyxl stated, "which is why we have infiltrated the cult on Muultar."

"Wait! You have people on the planet right now?" Reynolds asked. "In the cult?"

Xyxl nodded. "We do indeed. We have infiltrated them at the highest ranks."

"Oh…shit," Reynolds mumbled. "I need to reach out to my people on Muultar before something bad happens."

CHAPTER THIRTEEN

Asya removed the gag from Aht Gow's mouth and had started to untie her hands when the alien asked, "Why is *she* here?" it asked.

Asya paused, glancing over her shoulder at the alien, then back at the emperor's sister. The female's eyes nearly glowed with her fury, and she glared at the cultist who had given her the computer at the estate earlier.

"You...you...betrayer!" she shrieked. Despite being bound, Aht Gow tried her best to leap forward and attack the cultist. "I'll kill you, Kul Hu. You have betrayed our lord!"

"I'm guessing she's not one of your people?" Asya asked, realizing what was happening.

The cultist, Kul Hu, had the decency to look almost ashamed. He wouldn't meet Aht Gow's eyes.

"She is not, I'm afraid," the cultist answered. "She is one of the true disciples of Phraim-'Eh on this world; one of his most recent adherents."

"Which means she didn't know you had infiltrated them." Asya sighed.

"She did not," the alien confirmed. "At least, she *didn't* until a moment ago."

Asya groaned. "And here I was thinking we'd resolved all our problems."

Geroux raised her hand as if she were in school. "Uh, I'm very confused. Care to explain what's going on? I came here to swap hostages—the emperor's sister for you. Now I have no idea what's going on."

"I'm not sure I do anymore either," Asya admitted, returning the gag to Aht Gow's mouth while the female snarled and hissed. "I don't think we want to discuss it in front of her, though," Asya said, gesturing to the emperor's sister. "Let's bring San Roche and the Pod down here and stuff her inside for now."

Geroux groaned and started to argue, but Asya waved her off.

She gestured to the aliens. "Don't worry, these guys can see the Pod the same way they saw you when you showed up," Asya told her. "The only people who couldn't see it were these guys." She motioned to the fake cultists, who turned out to be husks of dead Muultu possessed by the energy of the alien beings to keep them from decaying, Asya explained.

A little disturbed by that idea, Geroux called San Roche down.

The Pod landed behind them a few moments later and Asya herded the emperor's sister inside, turning her over to San Roche for the time being.

Once the Pod's hatch had closed and Asya was sure Aht Gow couldn't overhear them, she started to explain.

"Zrrr here," she pointed to the nearest alien, "and that's Xuu," she said, indicating the other, "apparently followed Phraim-'Eh's cult to Muultar, much like we did. They've been around for about a year now, right?" Asya asked the aliens.

"That is correct," Zrrr answered. "We tracked several representatives of the cult to the planet after an attack on another world, Volora, in the Voloran System. Phraim-'Eh took over the planet shortly after and sent his minions out to conquer more. We arrived too late to stop them, so we chose to follow them instead."

"These people are taking over planets?" Geroux asked.

"It is their goal to turn them against the Etheric Federation or, at the very least, to provide the cult with supplies and soldiers for their war," Xuu explained.

"Chaos follows them everywhere they go," Zrrr said.

"And you are trying to stop that here?" Geroux asked.

"We are," Zrrr replied. "And beyond."

"Care to clarify?"

"We had hoped to infiltrate the cult at a remote location and introduce a sociological virus of a sort," Xuu told them. "This would allow us to perhaps contain and control the cult or, if nothing else, provide us with factual intel with which to decide on our course of action when dealing with them."

"And how did you hope to accomplish that?" Asya asked.

Zrrr wiggled a tendril in the direction of the church. "We provided the locals with access to a hidden communication tether through our agent Kul Hu. This allowed them to reach out to each other over vast distances, but it also provided us with access to their every message, since the tether is tied into our systems."

"That's why you showed up instead of the real cult when the signal was sent by Aht Gow," Geroux realized.

"Yes," Xuu told her. "We had to make her believe she was sending a message to Jora'nal, reporting your presence on the planet."

"Since Phraim-'Eh rules with fear, we had Kul Hu force her to do it to put the burden of your arrival on her shoulders rather than his, as would be expected. The computer he gave her to use was pre-programmed to direct the signal to us, not the cult. We did not, however, expect her to return here after she sent the message. She was to go back to the compound and await further orders."

"Except I kidnapped her and dragged her out here." Geroux sighed. "Sorry."

Asya grinned and patted her on the shoulder. "You did good."

"Absolutely," Ka'nak confirmed. "You snatched the emperor's sister and dragged her here to trade for Asya and me. Can't fault you for doing all that for us."

Geroux's cheeks reddened at the praise, but Asya could tell she was still bothered by what she'd done.

"You did the right thing," Asya assured her. "We'll figure it out from here, don't worry."

"Okay." Geroux sighed. "At least all this," she motioned to the church and the mountain at the back, then to the aliens and fake cultists, "explains all the Kurtherian energy signatures floating around this place."

The aliens stiffened, their electrical pulses stalling in their bodies.

"What Kurtherian signatures?" Zrrr asked.

Jiya had returned to the bridge after Reynolds disappeared. The crew filled her in on what happened, and her head spun.

"First the crew comes back to life, then these aliens snatch Reynolds off the bridge right out from under our noses? What other crazy stuff will happen?" Jiya asked.

"Those aren't the types of questions to ask unless you want to tempt fate," Maddox muttered. "Never tempt fate. She's spiteful on the best of days."

"Sounds like fate has already gone off the rails. Don't get me wrong, I'm glad everyone is alive and on their way to being well, but none of this makes any sense. Why would they take Reynolds, and why wouldn't he reach out to us?"

"Not that this is going to make you feel any better, but maybe he can't," Maddox said.

"No, that definitely doesn't make me feel better," Jiya admitted.

"These ships are moving fast," Ria exclaimed. "I'm able to keep up, but just barely."

"The fact that they allowed us close before going through the Gate makes it clear that they don't care if we follow them," XO explained. "Though it would have been nice to receive an invitation, or at least some indication that they're not going to turn around and start blasting again."

"The aliens didn't seem angry once they were able to communicate better with us," Ria stated.

"That doesn't make them our friends," Jiya argued. "These guys opened up on us as soon as we arrived, and they kidnapped Reynolds without warning. They apparently also have a history of attacking anyone else who comes to the planet. I'm not exactly sold on their goodness yet."

She turned to look at Tactical's station. She'd gotten used to seeing no one, the console empty, but she kind of wanted someone there to interact with directly and pictured a number of androids spread across the bridge. It would make everything so much easier.

"What are you looking at?" Tactical snapped.

And then he opened his mouth to speak again.

"Stay on high alert," she warned. "I don't trust these people."

"No shit, Sherlock," Tactical told her.

"I don't know if that's some Earth insult or you're becoming senile and can't remember my name, but now's not the time for it," Jiya returned.

"It never is," Comm added with a laugh.

"It's clear where they're going, people," Tactical went on. "You see those two ships out there?"

"You want us to follow them?" Jiya asked sarcastically. "You mean like we already are?"

The viewscreen flickered and a more detailed view appeared, overlapping the images of the ships. Energy signatures trailed behind them, disappearing into the distance, with another leading them.

"What the hell is that?" Jiya wondered.

"It's what Reynolds noticed when the two ships came after us," Tactical explained. "I don't know what you'd call it, but it's a kind of communication leash."

"A leash?"

"Best I can come up with," Tactical answered, and Jiya could practically hear him shrug. "The only reason we can pick it up is because it's similar to the frequency that the Loranian ship used to highjack Gorad's destroyers, although not the same, exactly. Reynolds followed the original signal back and plucked at pieces of the coding, which made it so we can adjust our scanners and detect it. This one is just close enough for us to see because it has hints of Kurtherian code attached to it. We'd have missed it if it hadn't."

"Wait, so you're saying these two ships here are remotely operated?" Jiya asked.

"That seems to be the case, based on this transmission," Tactical said. "Which means Reynolds is likely at the end of this beam."

"Given its trajectory, that would place him just off Mu," Ria stated, examining the numbers. "Right where—"

"At about the same coordinates as the alien ship we blasted," Tactical finished.

"They took Reynolds to the wrecked ship?" Jiya asked. "Why?"

Then it clicked.

"It wasn't that ship, but their command ship," she answered herself. "If these other ships are controlled remotely, that's probably their home base in this system. Tactical, replay the moment we fired the ESD."

The screen showed the attack on the enemy super-dreadnought.

"There you are," Jiya said, noting the shape behind their target.

"A second ship."

"That still doesn't explain why this leash thing is constantly visible, though," Maddox mused. "If it's a communication link, why is it so steady? Shouldn't it be active only when transmitting or receiving?"

"That why I called it a leash, since it appears that it's always on," Tactical replied. "It's not meant to be seen, though, and I doubt anyone else can track it because it would take an understanding of both Gorad's coding and the Kurtherians' in order for their systems to pick it out of the ether," Tactical explained. "We're able to see it because we've already dealt with both."

"We're closing on Mu," Ria reported. "The two alien superdreadnoughts are settling into a defensive position around their command ship."

"Any sign of weapons or shields being engaged?" Jiya asked.

"Weapon systems are not powered," Ria said, "and there is only standard shielding. They don't appear to be gearing up for war."

Jiya nodded. "Just keep watching them. I don't trust these guys."

"Incoming message," Comm called.

"About damn time," Jiya complained. "That has to be Reynolds, telling us what's going on. Patch him through."

"Uh, it's actually Geroux," Comm said.

"What? How?"

"You should probably ask her," Comm replied, opening the channel.

"Hey, Geroux," Jiya greeted her friend. "How are you managing to contact us way out here?"

"I'm hitching a ride on the alien communication network," Geroux answered.

"On the leash thing?" Jiya questioned.

"I have no idea what you're talking about," Geroux replied, "but there's a communication tether that reaches from the planet all the way up to the energy aliens' ships."

"Same thing." Jiya chuckled. "We were just discussing that very construct. It's kind of a creepy coincidence that you're bringing it up."

"It's more than that, I'm afraid," Geroux went on.

"What do you mean?" Jiya asked.

"The communication tether that the Gulg use—that's what the energy aliens call themselves—stretches between all of their ships, allowing for the small crew of Gulg on their command ship to control the superdreadnoughts and their other assets in the system."

"We already figured that out, tiny meatbag," Tactical sniped. "We've had our own run-in with the Gulg up here, so get on with your point before my circuits rust."

Geroux swallowed hard enough over the connection that Jiya heard her. "Well, it appears the beam has been hacked into and corrupted."

"How so?" Jiya asked.

"The Kurtherian energy signal that allowed us to pick up the tether on scanners and for Reynolds to track it to the *Pillar* back when they took over Gorad's ships? Well, that's not supposed to be there, according to the Gulg here on Muultar," Geroux explained. "It's how I'm reaching out to you, and a similar hack is how Jora'nal piggybacked on Gorad's remote signal to get his destroyers to come after us."

"Wait, you mean Jora'nal or some other cultist can access this beam to take over the remote alien superdreadnoughts?" Jiya questioned.

"Actually, I'm saying someone already has," Geroux stated. "The signal is being hijacked as we speak."

Jiya's gaze snapped to the viewscreen and zoomed in on the three alien ships hovering near the planet Mu. One of the superdreadnoughts was coming about in an unnatural manner.

"Gulg weapons coming online on that ship," Tactical shouted. "That superdreadnought is alive, people."

"Of course it is," Jiya groaned. "Battlestations!"

Aboard the Gulg command ship, Xyxl raised a hand to calm Reynolds. "There is nothing to worry about," he told the AI. "My people on Muultar have come across yours, and have explained the situation to them. Nothing untoward will occur."

"You don't know my crew," Reynolds replied with a laugh.

"My people are explaining the situation, and—"

Alarms sounded on the bridge, bathing the ship in a deep, ugly crimson.

"Nothing to worry about, huh? Famous last words," Reynolds snarked, shaking his head. "What's going on?

Eyes wide, Xyxl groaned. "We've lost control of one of our ships, and my crew cannot wrest command back," the alien explained. He trembled, surprise clear in his expression as he received a communication from his crew on Muultar, the sound a screeching crackle to Reynolds. "It appears there is some sort of malicious code attached to our communication tether, which connects our assets and allows us to control them from here."

Reynolds groaned. "It's that damn Kurtherian code," the AI remarked. "I noticed it earlier. That's what's doing this."

"There isn't supposed to be any Kurtherian coding connected to the tether," Xyxl stated. "In fact, our systems continue to read that there is nothing of the kind, and my crew cannot explain how our systems are being overwhelmed."

Reynolds started toward the nearest console to show them the coding, only to stop when he remembered the alien nature of the ship and its controls. He hadn't yet pieced together the vaguest idea as to how to operate any of the systems.

Instead, he transmitted the code into the air using a basic radio signal, so the Gulg could grab it and introduce it to their system on their own.

Before he could say anything about it, the wounded ship trembled as the first salvo of weapons fire from the controlled superdreadnought struck home. What little shields remained to the ship buckled and fell away under the merciless assault.

"Our defenses are down!" one of the aliens called.

"That signal I just sent contains a decryption program that will allow you to see the code they're using to highjack your systems," Reynolds announced, grabbing a console to keep from being knocked over.

When the enemy superdreadnought moved into a better attack position, Reynolds could only watch helplessly.

The second superdreadnought slipped between the two combatants, taking the blows meant for the wounded ship. Reynolds saw its hull flare and knew that if it had had atmosphere, it would be venting from the damage.

The *Qqhrt* engaged its engines and began to pull away slowly, warning sensors going off all over the bridge.

"This bucket is barely mobile," Reynolds commented, seeing the Gulg crewmembers frantically darting about the bridge, bouncing from station to station as they tried to keep the ship from being destroyed.

"We have little choice but to run, Reynolds," Xyxl said with a shrug. "We can fight this battle by proxy, but our weapon systems are down since our battle with you, as are our shields now. If we remain in place, it will take only one solid strike to lay us low."

"To kill us all, you mean," Reynolds corrected.

Xyxl nodded.

"Why not teleport us all to the other superdreadnought so we can fight directly?" Reynolds asked. "Better yet, why not send us to the enemy-controlled one so we can take it back?"

"Our transport system, while advanced, has its limitations," Xyxl explained as the *Qqhrt* fled. "In full defensive posture, the shields of the superdreadnoughts up and on alert, you would either re-form at the last instant, bounce off the shields, and end up floating in space, or the defensive barrier would tear your component molecules apart, leaving you little more than dust, incapable of being reassembled."

"I notice you only said *you*," Reynolds commented.

Xyxl shrugged. "Our shields are attuned to us. We can travel back and forth between our assets without issue."

"Then why don't *you* teleport over to your ship and fight from there?" Reynolds wondered.

"It would change nothing," Xyxl admitted. "We can operate the craft from here as well as we can aboard it. Besides, that first blow the enemy struck wounded the command ship since we were unprepared for such treachery and had not fully prepared its defenses before using it as a makeshift shield."

Reynolds looked back to the screen to see the defending superdreadnought continuing to take damage as it used its bulk to shield the fleeing *Qqhrt*.

"I've severed the communication tether," one of the other Gulg reported, although Reynolds couldn't tell which.

The controlled superdreadnought continued its assault, and the other SD looked to be getting the worst of their exchanges. Caught off-guard by the first attack, Reynolds understood it was fighting a deficit it would never recover from without creative assistance.

Another alarm sounded then.

"The Federation ship is closing on us," a Gulg reported.

Reynolds realized what needed to be done.

"Open a channel to my ship," he called. "And pack up

your databases as fast as you can, folks. We're getting out of here."

Xyxl stared at Reynolds for a moment before signaling to another of the Gulg to do as Reynold said. A comm channel was opened seconds later.

"Reynolds?" Jiya's voice rang out over the connection.

"No time for chit chat, Jiya," Reynolds told her, getting straight to the point. "What are the SD *Reynolds'* shields at?"

"Thirty-eight percent," she replied. "Why?"

Reynolds turned to look at Xyxl. "Will that do?"

The alien nodded.

"Just clear a spot on the bridge," he answered. "We'll be there in a minute."

"We?"

"Get ready to engage the superdreadnought that's firing on the others, but wait until we're aboard," he ordered, ignoring her question.

"Yes, sir," she shot back, all business.

Reynolds looked at Xyxl. "How much longer do you need?"

"A moment," the alien replied.

"The enemy-controlled ship has made it past our defending superdreadnought," a Gulg called. "We're being targeted."

"Now would be a good time to get out of here," Reynolds pressed.

Xyxl nodded. "I agree. Here we go," he warned.

Reynolds felt energy roll over him, and his vision went black for an instant, then cleared. When it did, he and the whole crew of the alien *Qqhrt*, all fourteen of them, stood on the bridge of the SD *Reynolds*, squeezed together into the forward section by the viewscreen.

"Little crowded here," Reynolds muttered, pushing past the energy forms of the Gulg and coming over to stand alongside Jiya, who stared wide-eyed at the gaggle of aliens now aboard the ship.

"That's...interesting," she mumbled, observing the aliens up close. They looked like storm clouds ready to explode.

"Target the active superdreadnought," Reynolds ordered.

"Like I haven't already," Tactical shot back.

"A moment, please," Xyxl said, separating from the other Gulg and coming over to Reynolds. "Unless you unleash that weapon you used to damage our command ship, you will do little damage to the superdreadnought before it realizes you have joined the battle and turns on your ship."

Reynolds raised a hand to keep Tactical from firing yet. "What do you suggest?"

Xyxl pointed to the viewscreen. "I have activated the *Qqhrt's* self-destruct mechanism, as well as that of the secondary superdreadnoughts—"

"And you aimed the *Qqhrt* at the ship," Reynolds realized, seeing the alien craft come about.

"It was all I could do," Xyxl admitted. "Once we severed the tether, we lost control of the remote ship."

"Uh, Captain?" XO cut in. "There's no way that lead ship is going to survive long enough for its self-destruct to be effective."

Reynolds stared at the screen and saw the controlled

SD blasting away at the already-damaged Gulg command ship. It was coming apart, and would never reach the enemy ship.

Then it exploded, going up in a flash that died as quickly as it tried to ignite.

The enemy ship turned away, undamaged by the explosion.

"They know we're here," XO announced. "The ship is headed our way."

Reynolds grunted, watching the enemy superdreadnought streak toward them. With the shields at less than forty percent, there was no way the SD *Reynolds* could take on the Gulg ship and win.

At least not head-on.

Jiya had the same idea.

"Bring us about so the deactivated SD is between us and the enemy ship, Ria," Jiya ordered. "And keep your distance. We don't want to get too close."

"Tactical, fire everything you've got at that ship," Reynolds ordered. "Piss these guys off and keep them coming at us."

Tactical complied and sent volley after volley at the ship. "I'm thinking they're going to do that anyway."

Reynolds turned to Xyxl. "Can you re-open your communication tether?"

"We can, but we risk—"

"Losing control of the only ship you have left, which is already under someone else's control?" Reynolds argued.

"There is more to it than that, I'm afraid," Xyxl stated. "That tether reaches all the way to our reserve ships at the edge of the system. I cannot reinstate the connection now that it is proven to be compromised."

"Son of a mother fuck!" Reynolds exclaimed. "I guess we have to do this the hard way. Target that wounded superdreadnought with everything we have short of the ESD, Tactical."

"On it!" Tactical answered, understanding what Reynolds intended.

The weapons fire shifted from the approaching craft to the superdreadnought that was dead in space. With its shields down, the railguns ripped into the hull of the craft, the salvo tearing through the armor as if it wasn't there.

The impacts pushed the ship in the direction of the other, Tactical driving it on with more weapons fire. The controlled SD rose to avoid colliding with it, seeming to slip clear of danger.

"Damn it!" Maddox howled, seeing it maneuver out of the path of the other ship.

Reynolds only smiled.

With its shields fully down, Reynolds had been able to scan the Gulg ship and determine when its systems would fail and the detonation would occur.

When the attacking Gulg ship bared its belly to the wreck beneath it, shields aimed forward to ward off attack, the self-destruct system initiated, engulfing both ships.

Reynolds sighed as the two craft were obliterated in the resulting explosion.

"Sorry to be the bearer of bad tidings, but you're going to need another ship, Xyxl," Reynolds told the alien.

CHAPTER FOURTEEN

Reynolds watched the explosion until it faded, the remnants of the two ships hurtling into space as so much junk and debris.

"Fortunately, I was able to summon our reserve ships before the tether was broken and before the *Qqhrt* was abandoned and destroyed," the Gulg replied. "They should arrive at Mu soon."

"Will you go to them?" Reynolds asked, unsure if he wanted the alien to say yes or no. He didn't completely trust the creature yet, but he felt there was much he could learn from him.

"My crew will travel to our base on Mu and wait to take control of the ships," he answered, "but I will remain to assist you and coordinate between our two peoples."

As if waiting for Xyxl to announce that, all of the Gulg but him vanished without a hint of how they had done it. The crew stared wide-eyed at where the group of aliens had just been.

"My people will reach out to me as soon as they have

taken possession of the replacement craft," Xyxl announced.

"Speaking of reaching out, we lost contact with Geroux when the tether shut down," Jiya reported. "She was hitching her signal to it to reach us, and now that it's gone…"

"Set a course back to Muultar," Reynolds ordered. "While we don't have to worry about her and the others mixing it up with the Gulg on the planet anymore, the cult is active on or near Muultar, and they know we're here, despite the Gulg's efforts."

"Course set," Ria replied. "Opening a Gate."

"Get us close, but not too close," Reynold warned. "We're not in any shape to step into a fight with Jora'nal and the *Pillar*."

"You thinking they're nearby?" Jiya asked.

Reynolds shrugged. "Possibly. It's not as if some backwater recruitment planet like Muultar would be handed top-end technology to pull this kind of move off. There has to be someone higher in the ranks pushing the buttons close by, and it stands to reason that it's Jora'nal since that prick has been shadowing us for a while now."

"That seems unlikely," Xyxl stated. "We have been monitoring the tether and intercepting all communications between the planet and their organization. We've kept them ignorant of the greater intentions of the cult and Phraim-'Eh by feeding them false information since we discovered them on the planet. There is no indication that there are any other cultists in the system to have done this."

"Yeah?" Reynolds asked. "How's all that worked out for you so far?"

Xyxl stiffened. Apparently he hadn't realized how compromised his system truly was.

He certainly did now that his ships had been destroyed.

"These people were able to hitch a ride on your beam without you knowing about it," Reynolds went on. "What else was going on that you didn't catch?"

Xyxl said nothing.

"Probably a whole lot," Reynolds said, answering for the alien.

"Jora'nal is dangerous *and* capable, and not to be under-estimated," Jiya stated. "His having hacked your tether means they've been monitoring your messages, as you have been theirs. It stands to reason that they have found another method of communication or the cultists wouldn't have known you were anywhere near the planet, given how simple their technology is. That means everything you know is compromised, simple as that. They've probably been feeding you as much crap as you have been them."

"Which means we can't trust the emperor or his people for sure now," Reynolds said.

"Krol Gow knew you were on Mu, Xyxl, standing in the way of their source of devium, and so did his inner circle. Any of those people could have been passing messages to the cult if they're part of this."

"That means our people on Muultar could be in danger, because they have no idea who they can trust," Jiya growled.

"We're through the Gate," Ria announced. "Maintaining safe distance from the planet. Shields and weapons up and ready."

"Reaching out to Geroux," Comm said, opening a channel.

"We've got a problem, Captain," XO chimed in.

"What the fuck is it now?" Reynolds snarled.

"Those low-rent cruisers of the emperor are currently in the process of assaulting the planet," XO told him.

"Are you seeing this?" Geroux asked over the comm.

"We are," Jiya answered, watching as the Muultu defense force was turned against the planet. "Looks like the cult has taken over all the ships at once. How are they doing that?"

"The Muultu systems are rudimentary," Reynolds said. "unlike Gorad's or the Gulg's. It's probably about as hard for them to take control of these things as it is to operate a calculator, which means they can take over all of them at once. That's what we're seeing, it appears."

"They might be garbage, but they still pack a healthy dose of firepower," Tactical said.

"What the hell is that one doing?" Maddox asked, pointing at one of the cruisers as it broke off its attack and dove straight into the atmosphere. "The one at the rear."

"Plot its trajectory!" Reynolds ordered.

"It's locked on a position outside of Ulf," Tactical responded. "Right where—"

"It's coming down right on top of us," Geroux shouted. "Shit! Get us out of here, San Roche!"

"Get us closer to the planet," Reynolds commanded.

Ria jumped on it, engaging the engines and sending the SD *Reynolds* streaking through space toward Muultar.

"They know we're here," XO warned. "Cruisers are turning on us. We're not up for a fight."

"You let these junkers hurt us, Tactical, and I'll plug you into one of the Pods forever, do you hear me?" Reynolds shouted. *"Forever!"*

"No pressure at all," Tactical mumbled. "Thanks, asshole."

Tactical drew more power to the shields as they advanced, meeting the small army of antiquated cruisers.

"Shields at fifty percent," Ria announced.

"It's going to have to do," Reynolds told her.

"I've got this," Tactical stated, the ship taking evasive maneuvers as the enemy cruisers fired on them. "Don't get your undies in a bind."

The nearest of the Muultu cruisers exploded moments later as a salvo of railgun fire tore through its engines as if its hull were made of paper.

"One down, seven to go," Tactical reported. "We're taking fire, but shields are holding."

"Now it's six," Geroux said over the comm, adjusting the count. "The ship that made a suicide attack just took out the cultist church out here on the outskirts of town."

"Are you okay?" Jiya spat.

"We're fine," Geroux told her. "We piled into the Pod and moved away before the cruiser hit, but the church, any evidence it might have held regarding the cult, and the Gulg's shuttle were all wrecked in the crash."

"Damn it!" Reynolds snarled. "It's like they're cleaning up their operations on the planet."

"Be careful up there," Geroux warned. "These cultists don't care about collateral damage."

"Why do you say that?" Jiya asked.

"Because we've got the emperor's sister with us," Geroux came back. "I, uh, kind of kidnapped her."

"You did what now?" Jiya sked.

"Well, it's a long story, but she's admitted to being one of the cultists and working under Phraim-'Eh. That didn't stop these guys from trying to take her out with a cruiser, though, so they don't care *who* they kill."

Jiya glanced at Reynolds, eyes wide, remembering the discussion about the cult having someone in the emperor's highest ranks.

He wondered if the emperor was involved too.

"Stay away from Ulf," Reynolds told Geroux. "We don't know what's going on, but the government is compromised to some degree. Until we can back you up and learn who all is involved, I don't want any of you near the place. I definitely don't want them realizing we've taken the emperor's sister hostage if they don't know already."

"I already sent a message to L'Eliana to have her cloak and retreat before things get worse," Jiya announced. "She's up and moving away from the landing field."

Another of the Muultu cruisers exploded as Tactical triggered a Gate and circled around behind the makeshift fleet to hit them.

A third ship was crippled before the others realized what was going on and dispersed to keep from being gunned down from behind.

"Four remaining," Tactical reported.

"Stay on them," Reynolds ordered. "XO, can you pinpoint that fucking Kurtherian hack signal and tell me where the hell it's coming from?"

"It's being obscured, bouncing around the planet as if

it's moving, but it's definitely coming from somewhere within the atmosphere," XO replied.

"From Muultar?" Reynolds asked for clarification.

"That's what I'm reading, but the signal is pulsing weirdly, fading in and out," XO called out. "Shit! Now it's gone. I've lost it."

Xyxl sighed loud enough to draw the AI's attention.

Reynolds turned his narrowed gaze on the alien. "You know something about this?"

The alien nodded. "The communication tether that tied us to the cult was part of a small escape craft that was hidden inside the mountain to the rear of the church. It served both as our way to feed the cultists information and also to provide our agents with a means of flight should they be discovered and need to slip away."

"And now the cultists are using it to control the Muultu cruisers," Reynolds snarled, realizing what was happening.

"It would appear so," Xyxl responded. "Fortunately, its range is limited. It needs to be close to initiate contact on its own when it's not being used as a receiver. Its energy source isn't very powerful."

"And now we've lost it?" Reynolds growled, glaring at XO's station.

"I'm doing long-range scanner sweeps to find it, but nothing so far," XO replied.

"Can you help us find it?" Reynolds asked the alien.

"The ship was not intended to be detected," Xyxl admitted, shaking his head. "With the tether down, there is no way for the vehicle to be tracked. Its cloaking is absolute."

"That's fucking wonderful," Reynolds complained.

"That means we won't know where it is until you reach out to it from your reserve ships, right?"

Xyxl shook his head. "We will not do so. That would leave us vulnerable to the cultists' control, since we have yet to determine how to avoid being contaminated by their foul programming. We cannot risk our last remaining ships in this system."

"So, you're saying we have to wait for the cultists to trigger the beam from the escape craft before we can pinpoint it?"

"That is correct, unless its occupants decide to deactivate the cloaking device."

"Which isn't going to happen, since the damn thing's been stolen and these guys don't want us blowing them out of the sky." Reynolds scoffed.

"With all of our people aboard your Pod, it would appear that is the likelihood," Xyxl confirmed.

Reynolds growled. "At least we'll know where they are when they take over another damn ship."

The alien remained silent, confirming Reynolds' suspicion that that was the only way they would find the missing ship.

Fucking fantastic!

"Any report from L'Eliana?" Reynolds demanded.

"She's nearly out of the city. She says the local alert broadcasts are reporting that the damage from the cruisers has been mostly limited to government installations," Jiya reported. "That was what the cruisers were firing at."

"So, there's a clear target, it seems," Maddox commented. "Although that throws the emperor's connection into doubt. Why attack his own assets?"

"Subterfuge?" XO suggested.

Maddox shrugged. "Maybe, but that seems a bit desperate, given their current situation."

Reynolds turned on Xyxl, frustrated that they were dealing with more of the hijacked ships. "Your entire system is questionable," he warned. "This is the second time they've used this tactic against us, but it's your technology that they're piggybacking on."

"One more down," Tactical announced.

"We must examine our processes to determine how they breached our security," Xyxl told the AI. "I will have my people begin work on that as soon as they reach out."

"I'd be happy to help you," Reynolds said with a wry laugh. "We have experience with this. All you have to do is give me access to your databases…"

Xyxl grinned. "As you so politely told me before, 'That's not going to happen.'"

Reynolds shrugged, smirking at hearing his own words flung back at him. "Was worth a try," he responded.

"Another one turned to dust," Tactical called. "Two left, and those guys are determined to get their ancient asses blown up."

"We both have secrets we would rather keep from each other, Reynolds," Xyxl told the AI. "I imagine our superiors would be most displeased if either of us overstepped our bounds and offered technology of the sort that might unbalance either side, however well-meaning our intentions."

"You can be sure of that," Reynolds told him, thinking of how Bethany Anne would respond to hearing that he had let some alien species get their hands on the full extent of the Federation knowledge.

It wouldn't be pretty.

"Still, I'd like to know how you kept doubling the power to your shields when we fought," Reynolds admitted.

Xyxl was quiet for a moment, then nodded. "I cannot provide you with the details of the process, but devium can be used to induce a short-term increase of energy. Our ships' systems have been adapted to use it for bursts of power and increased efficiency when needed."

"You use it like the Muultu do?"

"Our systems are more advanced and can process it more effectively, but yes, similar to the machines that they use to hold the toxic environment at bay," Xyxl answered.

"So, if we were to get some and—"

"L'Eliana is reporting that local troops are mobilizing in town, setting up a protective perimeter around the royal compound and other high-priority sites," Geroux announced over the comm, distracting Reynolds from his questioning. "Looks like martial law has been established. It also appears that we're taking the blame for everything."

"Of course we are," Jiya grumbled.

"Well, we *are* destroying their only source of planetary defense," Reynolds argued.

"Incorrect," Tactical shot back. "We *have* destroyed their only source of planetary defense. All of their cruisers are toast."

"I'm sure that news will be received well by the emperor," Reynolds griped.

"Fuck him," Tactical said. "What are the odds that his sister is involved in the cult and he isn't?"

Reynolds shrugged. "Who knows, but it looks like we're going to find out."

"You sure you want to go down there in the middle of all this chaos?" Maddox asked. "Why not just have the rest of the crew return to the *Reynolds* and wait it out? See what kind of message these people send us?"

"What does that get us?" Reynolds countered.

"It keeps our people alive, and it keeps those who've already died once on this trip from doing it again," he told him.

"He makes a compelling argument," XO said.

"He does, but that doesn't help us here," Reynolds replied. "We can't just abandon the planet to Phraim-'Eh and his cultists. They've attacked the city for a reason. I think we're obligated to find out why."

"Even if the emperor is in on it?" Tactical asked.

"Especially if he's in on it," Reynolds shot back. "WWBAD?"

"Say what?" Jiya asked, a single eyebrow raised.

"What would Bethany Anne do?" XO translated with a chuckle.

"She would probably drop down there on her own and proceed to kick everyone's ass who even looked as if they might be involved with Phraim-'Eh or his people," Reynolds stated unequivocally.

"She's got a thing for Justice, our Queen, that's for sure," Tactical muttered.

"We can't leave the Muultu trapped in the cult's web," Reynolds explained.

"I agree, but I thought your—*our*—mission was to hunt down and kill Kurtherians," Maddox questioned.

"These cultists are the philosophical descendants of the Kurtherians," Reynolds explained, telling him what Xyxl had revealed. "They are just as pervasive and deadly, if not more so, than the original Kurtherians. They have mimicked the Federation's efforts to expand and advance their organization, only they have chosen to do so at the cost of the free will and safety of the races they come across. We cannot allow it to continue, even if it means we place ourselves at risk once again."

The general raised his hands in surrender. "Looking for clarity, Captain, not a fight."

Reynolds nodded. He knew Maddox was playing Devil's advocate, and that was his role on the crew. The general was looking at all the options before them and working to steer Reynolds in the right direction by providing a counterpoint to his decisions.

Reynolds hated it, but he understood the man's tactics.

"So, you want us to prepare a crew to go dirtside?" Jiya asked.

The AI nodded. "Keep our people cloaked and outside of the city. We'll rendezvous with them once we're prepared, which should be shortly."

Reynolds turned to Xyxl.

"You'll come with us," he told the alien. "I presume you have some way to stay in contact with your crew once they retrieve the ships and reestablish connections besides the tether?"

Xyxl nodded.

"One that can't be hacked, preferably," Tactical added.

The alien grinned. "Yes, our private communications do not rely on the same system or transmit on the same frequency. If nothing else, this method of communication is secure."

"Good," Reynolds said. "I'm thinking we might need another ship or two at our back, given the condition of the *Reynolds*. Speaking of which…" The AI gestured to Comm. "Get Takal working on increasing the shield output, and have him oversee the remainder of the repairs. And see if he's figured out anything out about the radiation shielding while you're at it. We've been here much longer than expected already, and with our shields decayed, we can't risk adding radiation seep to the list of challenges on our plate."

"On it," Comm replied.

Reynolds turned to Xyxl. "Have your people contact Takal once they get situated. While the coding is different between our two ships, which means we can't simply transfer our hack defense to your systems, Takal knows enough to help your people get a handle on it."

"I will," the alien replied.

"Come on, Jiya," Reynolds said, waving his first officer on. "Let's get down there and see if we can clear all this up before it gets out of hand."

"Before?" Tactical questioned.

Reynolds shrugged. "Relatively speaking, of course."

Jiya chuckled and left the bridge, making her way to the Pod bay. Reynolds followed, and Xyxl floating along with them.

"This should be fun," Jiya commented. "Should we gather some troops?"

"Might be good to have a few on standby in case we need the cavalry to ride in, but if we show up with an army, it will make us look as if we're organizing a coup," Reynolds answered.

"If the emperor *is* involved, maybe that's a good thing," she fired back.

"We'll know soon enough if he is or not," Reynolds said. "Until then, we don't want to stir up any more shit than necessary."

"Yeah," Jiya muttered. "I think we've got more than enough shit to go around already, including the emperor's sister. As in, when are we going to give her back?"

CHAPTER FIFTEEN

On the planet, Reynolds decided to keep the risk to his people to a minimum, keeping them separated for the time being. He, Jiya, and Xyxl approached the emperor's secure location, intel from L'Eliana helping them find him. Asya, Ka'nak, Geroux, San Roche, and the other Gulg, along with the captive Aht Gow, remained in the cloaked Pod a short distance away in case they were needed. L'Eliana kept station alone in her Pod on the opposite side of Ulf, having settled in near the devium processing plant.

Reynolds and the others were met by a cadre of soldiers as soon as they made their presence known.

"Halt," one of the guards shouted, and a dozen weapons were pointed in their direction.

"Still think this was a good idea?" Jiya asked.

Reynolds shrugged. "If we're going to find out who's doing what and free these people from Phraim-'Eh, we've got to face the music."

Jiya grunted and raised her hands in surrender. "If by music you mean the firing squad, I'd rather not."

"We're unarmed," Reynolds announced. "We've come to speak to Emperor Krol Gow."

The soldiers approached, keeping them at gunpoint, and searched them. When they came to Xyxl, however, they had no idea how to proceed. They poked and prodded and scanned the alien as best they could, but they had no idea what they were looking for.

They gave in once they determined the creature didn't have any apparent weapons on his transparent frame, and then the soldiers bound their hands behind their backs and led the group into the building under continued guard.

They were ushered through a labyrinth of hallways until finally they descended a nondescript flight of stairs to a small chamber. The emperor and his council—all but Aht Gow, of course—sat huddled inside the sparsely furnished room, far from the comfort they were accustomed to. There was nothing but their seats.

The emperor leapt out his chair, scowling.

"You dare come back here after all you've done?" he screamed, cheeks flaring red with his anger. He stopped and stared at Xyxl, who, even in his humanoid shape, looked to be made of energy. "And who is that?"

Reynold went to raise his hands, only to remember they were secured by metal cuffs. He bit back a chuckle at the primitive restraints.

As if these things could really restrain me.

"Would we return and offer ourselves up so easily if we'd had anything to do with all this?" the AI asked, trying to reassure the emperor and ignoring the question about the Gulg.

"I have no idea what people such as you might do," he shot back.

"We are not your enemies," Jiya explained calmly. "Those people we told you about, the Cult of Phraim-'Eh, are responsible for what has happened here. They took over your ships and they struck at your installations."

"How is that even possible?" Krol Gow asked.

"We can explain it, but I'd rather not in front of your council," Reynolds stated matter of factly.

The male spun on his people, still furious, meeting the eyes of each before turning back to Reynolds.

"You challenge my council's loyalty?" Krol Gow growled.

"Only because I have information that makes me unsure who owns their loyalty," Reynolds replied.

The emperor stood stoically, saying nothing, arms crossed over his chest, breathing heavily.

"If it helps, our *mission*, the one we discussed, was a success," Reynolds added after a moment, speaking low to avoid everyone else hearing. The AI positioned himself so only the emperor could see his eyes and cast a furtive glance to Xyxl to make his point clear.

Krol Gow's expression darkened, then Reynolds saw realization there. He took another moment to contemplate before waving his council out of the room.

"Retreat to the hall for now, please," he said. "I would speak with our visitors alone."

Reynolds stared at the council as they were kicked out. To his surprise, none seemed overly fraught about it. They weren't happy, but none of them hesitated or found a reason to argue. They went quietly and without complaint.

Once they were gone from the room, and the guards had positioned themselves at the edges of the chamber, Krol Gow moved close so that only Reynolds, Jiya, and Xyxl could hear him. He eyed the alien.

"So, you are the beings who have kept us from the devium on Mu?"

There was both awe and anger in his eyes.

Reynolds was glad to see courage there, too.

Xyxl sighed. "It was not our intention to harm your planet or its people," the Gulg started. "Reynolds spoke to me about the devium ore, and while I understood your use of it, I did not understand your *need*. I was focused solely on my mission to rid the galaxy of the Cult of Phraim-'Eh and did not consider the negative impact of our actions as we defended our outpost on MU-2693. For that, I apologize, and we will, of course, allow you to return to your mining operations on MU-2693 without further issue."

Krol Gow stiffened, surprise replacing his fury. A second later, however, a flush returned to his cheeks, and he huffed.

"This cult you speak of has no place upon Muultar," he argued. "I have been offered no credible evidence of their existence, yet *you* have struck down several of my mining ships and cost many people their lives. *That* I can say for certain."

"The cult is real," Reynolds told him, "and they are here."

"My council has looked into it," he countered. "My sister investigated the issue herself and found nothing of this cult you speak of."

"Your sister is involved with them," Jiya said. "Of course, that's what she told you."

"What?" Krol Gow shouted, glancing around as if he expected to see Aht Gow standing there. "How dare you question—"

"That was why we wanted you to have your council leave the room," Reynolds explained. "She's admitted her involvement to my people. She's part of the cult we're warning you about."

"You know where she is?" the emperor snarled. He looked ready to wave his guards over to beat the answer out of them. "You must tell me now!"

"She's safe," Reynolds told him, wanting desperately to break his bindings and use his hands to urge the emperor to calm down, but he resisted. "We will return her unharmed, but you have to listen to us first, Emperor."

"You hold my sister hostage and expect me to kowtow to your demands?"

"Look," Jiya nearly shouted. "We don't *have* any damn demands. The only reason we're here is that the cult is a danger to you and your people. They are a danger to us! They don't give a damn about what happens to Ulf or Muultar or even your sister," she argued. "All they care about is creating soldiers for their war; cannon fodder for the mill. If Muultar gets destroyed in the process, so be it. This place means nothing to them."

Emperor Krol Gow started to pace in a tight circle. His soldiers inched closer, weapons at the ready, sensing his discomfort.

Reynolds hoped he could reason with the emperor and

not be forced to do something rash that would cause more harm than good.

"Remember when you promised you'd give me anything in exchange for your getting to return to Mu to mine your devium?" the AI asked.

Krol Gow stumbled to a halt and spun to glare at Reynolds. "I don't know if you are a fool or liquid courage runs in your veins, but you tread upon dangerous ground asking for anything when you hold my sister captive."

"All I ask is that you listen to us with an open mind," Reynolds went on. "Nothing more."

The emperor took a moment to contemplate what Reynolds was asking of him.

"And you will return my sister unharmed?"

Reynolds nodded. "I have no intention of hurting her or keeping her hostage," he said. "You can have her, but I need your assurance first that you will listen to us and take what we have to say seriously."

"I could have you killed where you stand," the emperor threatened.

"You most certainly can," the AI answered, playing the role of helpless victim to sway the emperor into listening. "There is nothing we can do to stop you."

Jiya swallowed hard at hearing that.

The emperor stared the three of them down for several long moments, saying nothing. Reynolds could see the uncertainty in the man's eyes. He doubted the emperor had ever been so directly challenged in his life, and he didn't know how to respond.

Reynolds pushed the subservient act further.

"I will have your sister delivered to you, and we will

remain under arrest as you discuss it with her," Reynolds told him. "Should you not believe us after that, you can execute us and we will not fight it."

"Uh, thanks," Jiya grumbled. "Do I get a say in this?"

Reynolds ignored her.

"You place me in a difficult situation, Reynolds," Krol Gow said, shaking his head.

"You and me both," Jiya mumbled.

"I know that, Emperor," the AI agreed. "I promised you we would resolve your mining problem on MU-2693, and we have. I am a being of my word. And now I promise that your people are in danger from another source, the cult. My crew and I, and the Gulg, wish to help rid you of that problem as well."

"What could these people, these cultists, possibly want from Muultar?" the emperor asked. "Why would you think my people would give in to such foolish propaganda that they would turn on their ruler and their fellow citizens?"

"The cult knows that Muultar will die without the devium," Reynolds stated. "What better reason to rebel against a leader who has not informed them of their impending demise?"

Krol Gow's eyes went wide, and he gasped.

"Who else knew about that?" Jiya asked.

The emperor didn't want to answer. It took him several long moments before he finally admitted, "Only the council and...Aht Gow."

Jiya raised an eyebrow as if saying, "I told you so."

Reynolds went on, "Your sister has told the cult everything she knows, Emperor. They are using that information to sway your people and build the foundation of revolt among your citizens. They attacked your city with your own ships to bring them to their side."

"But they struck only royal installations," Krol Gow argued. "Why would people fear that since we informed them of such?"

Jiya couldn't help but chuckle. "You mean, the government told them that only government installations were attacked? The same government that has kept their coming doom from them?"

The emperor covered his mouth and stared at the first officer. Reynolds could see realization creeping into his eyes and decided it was time to push harder.

"They were likely trying to kill you, Emperor—you and your council. That was why they attacked your installations," Reynolds continued. "Who would sit upon the throne were you to die?"

"My…sister," Krol Gow managed to choke out. "Aht Gow would become empress."

He stood stiff as a board, reining in his panicked breaths at the thought.

"Wouldn't that make things easier?" Jiya commented sarcastically.

"And she wasn't with you when the attack happened, was she?" Reynolds pushed.

"No, but *you* have her," he fired back. "You could have captured her before then."

Reynolds nodded in agreement with the emperor's logic. "She could have been, and technically she was. However, we did not take her from your compound. She left on her own, slipping past your gate guards, and covered herself in loose garb that hid her identity.

She then traveled to an estate on the other side of Ulf."

"You can check with your soldiers at the gate, and we can show you the home she visited," Jiya added.

"Do you remember seeing her after we were escorted to the guest quarters?" Reynolds asked.

"Yes! She was with me until I went to—" The emperor paused, remembering. "Until I left to show you the devium-processing plant." He drew a sharp breath. "She was not here when I returned."

"And the rest of the council?" Jiya pressed. "Were they?"

He thought for a moment, then nodded. "They were. All of them," he admitted. "They hadn't left the compound."

The emperor turned and examined his soldiers, his gaze drifting over the mass of them as they crowded around the walls, eyes narrowed in suspicion.

"How can I trust anyone now?" he asked, looking back at Reynolds.

"You can't," the AI responded. "Not until you rid your planet of the Cult of Phraim-'Eh and its influence."

"But how?" he asked. "I have seen no evidence of its influence, as I already told you. I know nothing of it."

Reynolds gestured to Xyxl. "The Gulg have been here for nearly a year, ever since they took over Mu," he told the emperor. "They have infiltrated the cult's upper echelon and hidden among them. There is a church where they meet in the toxic wastes outside of Ulf, and who knows how many other places across the planet?"

"If they could turn your own sister against you, imagine what they have done to your people," Jiya said, trying to press the emperor into believing them.

"From what we can gather, the cult is small now," Xyxl said. "Our agents have identified less than fifty of your citizens across the planet who are involved as of yet. That number, however, is suspect, since the cult has shown that it knows of our presence, both in the system and on Muultar."

"So, you're telling me you have no idea how many of these cultists there are in Ulf, let alone on Muultar?" the emperor railed. "How many of my people could have submitted to them?"

"Unfortunately, that's true. We don't know, which is why we need your assistance," Reynolds said. "We have been unable to investigate the true scope of the cult's influence here to date since it was revealed that the Gulg's presence here had been sussed out, likely by your sister. There is no certainty that any of what the Gulg have learned has any value."

The emperor started to pace again, but this time Reynolds could tell it was from worry, not anger. The Muultu leader was struggling to make up his mind what to do. He was beginning to believe that his sister had betrayed him, and the thought sickened him.

"If what you say is true," he finally said, stopping in front of Reynolds, sweaty and pale, "what would you have me do?"

"Help us chase them from the planet and ensure that no more of the cultists or their philosophy can take root here," Reynolds stated plainly. "You will be saving far more than just your own people by doing so."

"And what do *you* gain from this?" Krol Gow asked. The suspicion remained on his radiation-tortured face.

"We came here chasing this enemy, as we told you initially," Reynolds answered. "Your support would deal them a blow that might lead to their absolute destruction. That's what we gain from it."

The emperor drew a slow, deep breath, his gaze wandering the room. He had yet to be convinced.

But as he contemplated, there was a loud *thump* against the door and some scrambling with the handle. It was flung open a second later. Several soldiers stormed into the room, stirring the ones already there into a frenzy. The council darted in behind the soldiers, eyes wide with panic.

"We're under attack!" one of the soldiers shouted.

CHAPTER SIXTEEN

"What's going on?" Krol Gow asked the guard, his voice raw with emotion.

"The people are rebelling, my lord," the soldier reported. "They have risen up and are attacking the royal compound, as well as many of our other installations." The guard was out of breath, huffing as he spoke, but he kept on. "Hundreds of them are making their way toward us now, blocking the roads and cutting off the escape routes from the building, my lord. We need to leave."

"I saw them myself," one of the council members, Chae Dun, announced, her eyes wide with terror. "They are armed, my lord."

Asya came over the comm. "You guys need to get the hell out of there. Now!" she barked. "You've got an army of people moving toward you, and they're gonna be on top of you in just a few moments. Want me to slow them down?"

"No," Reynolds barked, understanding that she meant firing on the people. "Do not engage the crowd. That's a last resort only."

Jiya looked at him, shaking her head. "These people are cultists now, Reynolds," she told him. "You sure you want to hold back? They won't be offering us the same kindness."

"I'm sure we do for now," he answered. "We didn't come here to kill everyone. If we can find a way to show these people that Phraim-'Eh is using them and taking advantage, maybe we can save them."

"*Maybe?* That's a lot of faith to put in one word," she grumbled as she watched the frenzy of motion in the small room.

"Maybe," the AI said, chuckling when he realized what he'd said. "No pun intended."

L'Eliana reported in then. "I have to pull away from the devium plant," she said. "A large group of Muultu is attacking it and destroying the place. Should I try to stop them?"

Reynolds told her not to bother. The cultists were tearing the city apart, and there was little he could do to stop them.

That frustrated him to no end.

He turned to the emperor then.

"We have to get you out of here before these people arrive and start tearing this place apart. Have your troops form up and come with us."

To Reynolds' surprise, the emperor didn't hesitate.

"On me," he commanded, and his soldiers grouped around Krol Gow and the crew and council.

Reynolds didn't completely trust the council, thinking one or more of them might be in collusion with the cult or

Aht Gow, but if he had to guess by the horrified looks on their faces, none of them had expected this.

"Free these people," the emperor ordered.

"No need," Reynolds replied, shrugging, and easily broke the chains that bound his hands together. He ripped the shackles off his wrists and tossed them aside.

Jiya, still in her powered suit, did the same. The cuffs simply fell off Xyxl as he adjusted the shape of his hands, sharpening them to points, then returning them to humanoid shape and function.

The emperor stared, realizing they could have done that at any time.

Reynolds didn't give him time to think about it. Having memorized the way in, the AI led them from the room and back through the winding corridors to the exit. They hit the doors a minute later and spilled out into the street.

The sound of a wild mob struck them as soon as they were outside.

Screams and bloodthirsty shouts rang out, and Reynolds could smell smoke lingering in the air. A distant black cloud hovered over the city somewhere in the direction of the royal compound. Reynolds was sure the building was engulfed in flames.

Although he wasn't sure how the hell that could be the case, given that everything here was made of stone or steel.

There wasn't time to contemplate it, though. The mob was almost on them.

"Oh..." the emperor sputtered after the frothing crowd shrieked at him when they saw him emerge from the building.

The throng roared and pressed forward. Weapons fired, blasts of energy tearing the nearby walls apart.

Jiya gave Reynolds a knowing look as they ushered the emperor away from the building and down one of the few open streets.

"Not too late for me to give you some breathing space," Asya suggested from the Pod, hidden somewhere above.

"The answer's still no," Reynolds replied, running from the crowd with the emperor, the council, and the group of soldiers at their backs.

"Here if you need me," Asya offered. "Though I have to say, this part of town is pretty tightly packed. There's no place nearby for me to set down if you want to hitch a ride."

"Understood," Reynolds told her. "We're on foot for now." He waved the emperor and his people on. "This way," he said, darting down streets and alleys, using the connection to the Pod's scanners to plot the best route away from the charging cultists.

The royal guard didn't have the same restraint as Reynolds. They snapped off shots as they ran, desperate, sloppy attacks that plowed into the crowd indiscriminately.

That wasn't going to help their cause with the people, but Reynolds wasn't going to tell the emperor's guards how to protect him. At the end of the day, they'd have to deal with that fallout on their own. Right now, Reynolds' only concern was getting Krol Gow someplace safe.

It wasn't going to be easy.

The fringes of the mob had caught up with them and were throwing themselves at the soldiers.

A person screamed as he was dragged down by the people. Fists and feet pummeled him, and he was left bleeding and groaning as his attackers raced toward another victim.

Unfortunately, they found Jiya instead.

A male clawed at her shoulder, trying to bring her down, but the first officer was having none of that.

She grabbed the man's wrist and twisted, and there was a loud *snap* as she flung his arm over her head and threw him to the ground.

The next cultist took the opportunity to swing at her. Jiya dodged the blow and spun, slamming her knee into the person's midsection.

He huffed like a bellows, all the air in his lungs driven out, and he bent over in pain. Jiya followed up with a brutal uppercut that crushed his jaw and sent him flying into the cluster of shouting people behind him.

She spun back and rejoined the fleeing group.

"There are way more of these folks than I thought there'd be," she admitted, casting a furtive glance over her shoulder to see the still-advancing crowd.

"It goes to show you just how busy Phraim-'Eh's people have been down here," Reynolds said, his head on a swivel as he plotted their next move.

Xyxl nodded. "They were feeding us as much disinformation as we were them." The alien sighed. "Likely more, from the looks of it."

"This cult might seem simple on the surface, but their leadership is far from it," Reynolds told the alien. "Much as I hate to admit that. They've gotten ahead of us a number of times already."

"And they're going to do it again if we don't figure something out," Jiya complained, looking at the crowd again.

"We need to separate," the AI suggested. "We're too big a group to slip away unseen. We can't move quickly or quietly."

"I can lead them away," Jiya offered, but Reynolds shook his head.

"No, I need you with me," he told her.

Two more cultists caught up to them, and the soldiers spun and gunned them down.

That did nothing to deter the rest of the throng. Everyone pushed forward, overwhelming the pair of soldiers who'd slowed to fire.

Reynolds darted down an alleyway, dragging the emperor's entourage with him.

"The soldiers have to go," the AI snarled.

Krol Gow looked at Reynolds uncertainly on hearing the AI's statement. He didn't want to be without his guards.

"These people are proving their loyalty to me," Krol Gow said. "I cannot leave them behind."

"I understand," Reynolds replied, "but they are also going to be the death of you." There was a coldness to his voice that made the emperor shudder.

Krol Gow looked at his council, who were huffing and puffing and then at his soldiers, who clustered around them in their royal uniforms, making them stand out no matter how chaotic the crowd at their heels.

The emperor gave a reluctant nod.

Reynolds understood his concerns, but right then the soldiers were more of a liability than a help.

"There are a pair of intersections up ahead," Reynolds offered. "We part ways there, your soldiers pausing to make a quick stand, then running to the north while we go south."

"That takes us deeper into the city," the emperor explained, swallowing hard at the plan.

"Which is the last place the throng would look for you," Reynolds told him.

Krol Gow sighed but nodded, realizing Reynolds was right.

"My people will do what they must," the emperor said, the words barely loud enough to be heard.

He called one of his soldiers over and relayed the order.

The soldier didn't hesitate in his response. "Yes, my lord." He snapped a salute, striking his chest with his fist, and returned to the soldiers to relay the order.

A number of soldiers had sour looks on their faces when they heard what was expected of them, but none wavered. They offered nods to the emperor, who returned them mournfully.

Reynolds felt bad for both the soldiers and the emperor, but there was little he could do without killing too many Muultu.

Then he realized there *was* something he could do.

It wouldn't stop the rushing mob, but it might slow them down.

"You have eyes on us?" the AI asked Asya.

"I do," she came back right away. "What's up?"

"I'm sending a target to the Pod's systems," he answered. "On my mark, fire on it."

"Yes, sir," Asya replied without hesitation, glad to finally be doing something besides watching the crew get chased.

Reynolds told the emperor, "We're almost there. Have your people form up right before the intersection, packed tightly to obscure the view of what's behind them, and then fire at the ground ahead of the crowd to slow them down."

The emperor groaned. "Many of my people will die today."

"Fewer than if the cult usurps your planet," Reynolds countered. "We'll keep the body count to a bare minimum, I promise."

Krol Gow nodded, accepting his fate. The council agreed without argument.

They came to the intersection then, and Krol Gow signaled his men. A soldier barked an order, and all of them spun and skidded to a halt, weapons aimed at the road. They let loose a barrage of fire that tore the street up, kicking up debris and dust and causing the mob to hesitate.

Reynolds, the crew, the emperor, and his council ducked, staying out of sight in the chaos, and darted south down a dark alley.

As soon as they were gone, the soldiers made a show of breaking off and racing north loudly, feet stomping and voices raised.

"Now!" Reynolds ordered.

Asya reacted instantly.

She fired a blast from the Pod, ripping into the building nearest the intersection. The wall exploded and collapsed in a clatter of stones and steel, debris tumbling down like an avalanche and spilling onto the street with a rumble.

Screams rose from the mob, and they stumbled to a stop ahead of the bouncing wreckage.

"Direct hit," Asya reported from above.

Reynolds pushed the group faster, taking another quick turn a block later and leading the group deeper into the bowels of the city.

"That'll buy your soldiers time to scatter and find someplace to hide," Reynolds assured the emperor.

The AI knew for a certainty then that the emperor wasn't involved and simply acting. He cared too much about his people to have sacrificed them to Phraim-'Eh and his cult.

"The crowd's starting over the rubble," Asya reported.

Reynolds turned down another alley and waved the group on, waiting for the final confirmation of whether or not the ploy had worked.

He got it a moment later.

"The mob has turned north, following the soldiers," Asya called over the comm.

Jiya grinned and gave Reynolds a thumbs-up.

"Now let's find some place to hide the emperor and council where they'll be safe," Reynolds told her.

He turned to Krol Gow.

"Is there somewhere near here where your people would never expect you to be?" the AI asked.

The emperor nodded. "There is an area of town near the atmospheric shield that has been abandoned due to a weakening in the barrier. It is entirely empty of people, and no one would go there due to the higher levels of radiation seeping through the defensive screen."

Chae Dun gasped. "You would take us to the barren zone? What of the radiation?"

"We only need to be there for a short time, Chae," the emperor explained. "That is correct, right?"

"It is," Reynolds confirmed.

The female didn't look convinced, but there wasn't time to argue. Reynolds needed to get the council and the emperor to safety.

"The wastes it is," the AI said. "Lead the way, Emperor. We'll find someplace better once we know all of you are safe."

Krol Gow motioned for the others to follow and the group started off again, headed toward the other side of Ulf.

As they went, the comm came alive with Maddox's voice.

"We have a bit of a problem up here," the general reported.

"A *bit* of a problem?" Jiya asked.

"I might be underselling it some," Maddox replied.

"Sitrep," Reynolds ordered.

"We found out where the Gulg shuttle is," he answered.

"And that's a problem?" Reynolds countered.

"Well, it is, because we only found it because it activated the communication tether," Maddox said.

"Are there any ships in the area they can take control of?" Reynolds asked.

"In the area? No, but that's kind of the problem,"

Maddox answered. "The beam is pulsing strongly and has reached out past us…toward Mu."

Reynolds stumbled to a halt as realization washed over him.

"Oh, *shit.*"

"Exactly." Maddox groaned.

CHAPTER SEVENTEEN

Once Reynolds and the crew had reached the wastes of Ulf and found a remote, empty building to hide the emperor and his council, he, Xyxl, Jiya, and L'Eliana returned to the SD *Reynolds* in one of the Pods.

They'd left Asya and the others behind on the planet in the remaining cloaked Pod. The AI had parked them near the emperor and his people, letting Asya, Geroux, Ka'nak, San Roche, and the remaining Gulg guard the emperor in case someone stumbled across their hiding place.

There were too many people in the Pod already, and Reynolds didn't want to risk bringing the emperor to the *Reynolds* with him since he was certain there was trouble coming.

On the bridge, Reynolds spun on Xyxl. "I thought you said the shuttle had a short-range device only."

"It does," the alien assured him. "I'm not certain how Phraim-'Eh's people were able to… Oh."

Reynolds realized the answer at the same time the alien did.

"The devium," they said in unison.

"They're using the ore to increase the power of the hacked signal," Reynolds went on.

Jiya grunted. "That explains why they want the planet so badly. Now that they have one of your ships, they can reverse-engineer the system and use the tether to wreak all sorts of havoc using your tech."

"We need to take out that shuttle," Reynolds snapped. "Can we still track it?"

"It has circled around Muultar," Comm reported.

"Then go get it," Reynolds ordered.

"That's going to have to wait," Comm stated coldly.

Proximity alarms sounded then, the bridge turning red. Reynolds muted the sirens and grunted.

"Let me guess, a Gulg superdreadnought just Gated in." Reynolds grimaced.

"You must be psychic," Tactical answered. "The communication beam is linked to it."

"Enemy weapons are online, and we're being targeted," XO called.

"Of course, we are," Reynolds scoffed. "Shields to full, evasive maneuvers."

The first burst of energy weapons rattled the *Reynolds* as the enemy ship opened fire.

"Where do we stand?" the AI asked.

"Takal managed to get our shields back up to eighty-five percent by using the small store of devium Jiya managed to bring back to the ship," XO reported. "It's inefficient, however, since the ship's systems have not been adapted to use the ore properly. Takal worked up some jerry-rigged processor to power the shields, but the ore is limited on top of the inefficiency."

"Any good news?" the AI asked.

"I saved fifteen percent by switching to Geico?" Tactical offered.

"The enemy superdreadnought is closing on us," Ria reported.

"That's the *Vvvor*," Xyxl clarified.

"Is there any way to shut that damn tether off?" Reynolds asked Xyxl.

The alien shook his head. "Outside of destroying the source, no. My people have yet to ascertain how these cultists are corrupting our systems. They seemed to have learned how to hide their efforts better since your last encounter with them."

"Why can't we fight dumbasses?" Tactical asked. "Smart enemies suck hamster tails."

"Takal to the bridge!" Reynolds ordered over the comm. "Now!"

"Already on my way," the old inventor replied, out of breath.

Reynolds needed him and the Gulg to get back to work on the hacking defense. Between the inventor, the aliens, and his other personalities, Reynolds figured they could eventually understand how to shut down the remote access and return control of the ship to the Gulg.

He just needed to do it before it was too late.

"I'm firing back, but that SD has got one hell of an energy rating," Tactical announced. "Weapons aren't doing shit to it."

Reynolds examined the console before him, reading the scanner reports. "They've powered up the ship."

"That was actually us," Xyxl admitted sheepishly. "We believed ourselves safe at such a distance and wanted to be prepared should we need to show up and defend against other ships the cult might have in play. Both the *Vvvor* and the *Xzzt* are using their stockpile of devium to increase the power of their systems."

Reynolds grimaced. "This is one hell of a comedy of errors, except I'm not fucking laughing." He shook his head and stared at the viewscreen, seeing the Gulg superdreadnought closing.

"What about your other ship?" the AI asked. "Do you still control it?"

Xyxl nodded. "It seems the cult is incapable of taking over more than one of our craft at a time."

"Or that's what they want us to believe," Jiya added.

Reynolds grunted his agreement of her assessment.

He had no idea what the cult was capable of. They had known what they were doing by stealing the hidden—*shittily so*—Gulg shuttle, and they had known about the increase in power that could be gained by using the devium.

What else do they know?

That thought haunted Reynolds.

The cult had been one step ahead of them from the start, and it was pissing Reynolds off.

"I'm getting sick and tired of these assholes," the AI snarled.

"You and me both," Jiya added.

"I was sick of them first," Tactical called.

"Not a competition," XO told the other personality.

"Of course, it's not," Tactical answered, "because I've already won."

"Shields are down to seventy percent," Ria reported.

"Any luck getting past their defenses?" Reynolds asked Tactical.

"I might have scratched the paint on that last salvo," Tactical replied.

"I'll take that as a no," Reynolds replied.

"Should I summon my other craft?" Xyxl asked. "My people are waiting for orders."

Reynolds looked at the attacking enemy ship as the SD *Reynolds* shuddered under yet another barrage of fire. Bursts of energy flared against the gravitic shields, and Reynolds could see that some of the railgun shots were punching through already.

Fortunately, there'd been no reports of injuries or deaths from the crew.

The AI had never been indecisive, but there were so many factors that he was forced to take a moment to consider them all. So few of their options appeared viable, let alone like good moves.

"Yes, bring your ship to us," Reynolds told the alien as yet another attack thundered over the *Reynolds'* shields.

"What if they take over the other ship when it arrives?" Maddox asked.

"If they were capable of doing it, it makes sense they would have already," Reynolds replied. "We've already proven we can hold our own against the Gulg ships one on one, so if Jora'nal or whoever is running all this wanted to take us out, they would have activated both ships if they were capable."

"Lots of assumptions in that," Tactical argued. "You know what they say about assuming."

"Well, you always make an ass of yourself, Tactical," Reynolds fired back. "I certainly can't make it any worse."

"Shields are down to fifty percent," Ria called out. "We're getting battered."

"Bring up the ESD?" Tactical asked.

Reynolds shook his head. "We don't need to blow out the last of our systems unless we no longer have a choice."

"I'll warm it up, just in case," Tactical said.

"Second Gulg SD incoming," Ria announced. "It's turning its weapons on the other ship."

"Finally, some good news." Jiya laughed.

"Asya, I'm sending you that shithead shuttle's coordinates," Reynolds called over the comm. "I want you to go put a boot up their ass. A couple of boots."

"You want us to leave the emperor alone?" she asked.

"Any signs of people in the area?"

"Scans show the area is clear…for now," Asya replied.

"Then yes," the AI told her. "The shuttle is the priority. We need to get that damn signal shut off. Blow those fuckers apart."

"On it," Asya answered in a low and dangerous voice, the comm going silent immediately after.

The bridge doors hissed open, and Takal shuffled in as quickly as he could. He went straight to a console and plopped down, getting to work.

"Working on the breach, sir," the old inventor muttered, not taking his eyes off his station. "It's a stubborn one."

Reynolds motioned to Xyxl. "Help coordinate with your people. XO, Comm, Helm, you three do what you can to assist."

Sour affirmatives followed.

The second Gulg superdreadnought, the *Xzzt*, opened fire on the first as it came in on its starboard flank and tore at its shields, forcing the enemy to pull power from its forward defenses to resist the assault.

"Give them what you've got," Reynolds ordered.

Tactical unloaded on the enemy ship and whooped when a number of his shots pierced the shields and struck home.

They did little more than scar the hull, but it was the most effective they'd been since the engagement began.

And then shit went sideways.

The *Xzzt* turned on the *Reynolds* and blasted it, ripping up a section of the hull and forcing the bots to go to work as atmosphere vented from the wound.

"What the absolute fuck?" Reynolds shouted. "Bring us about to face that other ship."

"The signal was turned on the *Xzzt* when it came around behind us," Jiya reported.

"Damn it!" Reynolds snarled. "It's good to know they can only control one ship at a time, but we can't keep both of them off our ass if they're hopping back and forth between them."

The *Vvvor* turned its guns on the *Xzzt* a moment later, driving the other superdreadnought back.

"I have crew on both ships, so we're capable of regaining control as soon as the communication tether is redirected," Xyxl announced.

"Which means there's no winning this fight without killing some of your people," Reynolds growled.

"If there is time, my people will teleport to the winning craft," the alien assured him.

That didn't make Reynolds feel better about it, but he couldn't risk his crew getting killed by treating the controlled ships with kid gloves.

"How's it going out there, Asya?" he asked.

"It's like playing tag with a lightning bolt," she came back. "That ship is fast as hell and way more maneuverable than we are."

"It was designed as an escape craft," Xyxl told her. "It has very little in the way of weaponry, but it is quite fast. The constant use of the tether, however, should slow it down somewhat."

"Not much difference between a fast lightning bolt and a slow one," Asya remarked. "This Pod isn't designed to run a craft like that down."

"Going to have to play it smarter," Reynolds stated. "Launching two more of the Pods to see if we can cut off its movements. Go get those assholes, Ria."

"I'll try. Coordinating with Asya," the ensign answered as soon as the Pods were away. "We'll see what we can do."

"There is no try," Reynolds told Ria.

"The *Vvvor's* hitting us again, damn it!" Maddox called. "This back-and-forth shit is giving me whiplash."

"It's giving the ship more than that," XO warned. "There have been no casualties yet because I've ordered the crew away from all non-essential areas of the ship, but it will only be a matter of time."

Reynolds hoped Xyxl could do what he did the last time

the crew had been killed, but that wasn't something he wanted to rely on.

They'd yet to examine the people who'd been returned to life to see if there were any long-term or dangerous side effects from what the Gulg had done.

More blows struck the ship then, and Reynolds cringed as damage reports filtered through, listing a number of injuries.

We might not have a choice soon, he thought.

"We're getting torn up," Tactical complained. "Every fucking time I reinforce the shields one direction, we get smacked from the other. There's no way to provide even coverage without us getting fucked from both sides."

"I can't get us away from them, sir," Ria reported. "The two ships are being maneuvered too well for us to avoid them."

"Glad you wanted that second ship nearby, Reynolds," Tactical sniped.

Reynolds contemplated plugging Tactical into the Jonny-Taxi body so he could kick his ass, but that idea, however satisfying, was fleeting.

Tactical was right. It *had* been a mistake bringing the second Gulg ship there.

Reynolds hadn't anticipated the speed at which the beam could switch between ships.

"Xyxl, tell your crew to—"

"I think we've got something!" Takal called, excitement making his voice raw.

Either that or he'd been drinking.

"Spit it out, man!" Reynolds shouted.

"We've been able to isolate the foreign coding that we

think is responsible for providing remote access to the Gulg ships."

"Then fucking excise that shit!" Reynolds shouted.

"Working on it," the inventor replied, sweat beading his brow.

"Work faster," Tactical urged.

Another salvo of enemy fire slammed into the *Reynolds*.

"We've lost an engine," XO called.

"Shields at twenty-two percent and dropping," Ria reported. "Twenty…nineteen…"

"If you've got something for us, Takal, now would be the time to whip it out," Reynolds barked.

"There!" Takal announced, jabbing a button on the console and leaning back to watch what happened.

The *Reynolds* trembled as another round of weapons fire battered the hull. Another round followed.

"Eight percent," Ria called, her voice quavering.

The *Vvvor* filled the viewscreen, its weapons readying to fire again.

"Doesn't look like it worked," Reynolds said softly.

Silence overtook the bridge as the enemy ship drew closer.

CHAPTER EIGHTEEN

The *Xzzt* went after the *Vvvor*, unleashing its entire arsenal.

The *Vvvor*'s shields dropped just before impact and the superdreadnought was eviscerated, explosions rippling through its guts and tearing outward, throwing off showers of debris in every direction.

Reynolds sighed in relief, then remembered that there were Gulg aboard the exploding ship.

"Did your people—?" he started to ask.

Xyxl nodded. "They were able to reach the *Xzzt* before the *Vvvor* went up since I was able to warn them as to what was coming."

"You guys shut down the shields?" Jiya asked.

"We did," Xyxl said, patting Takal on the shoulder.

"Why didn't you just shut it down?" she continued.

"The *Vvvor* was already in the process of firing, and there was nothing short of its destruction that would stop it from doing so," the alien said, a hint of sadness to his voice. "Had we chosen to act differently, the *Reynolds* would have been destroyed along with the *Vvvor*."

"Tough choice," Maddox muttered.

"It was the right one to make," Xyxl stated.

"Sorry to be the bearer of bad tidings," Takal interrupted, "but we're not out of this yet."

"Report!" Reynolds ordered.

"We have been able to disrupt the signal for a few moments, but it's a temporary fix," the inventor said. "The enemy is already working to counter it, and may be back into the Gulg system any second now."

"And here I was getting ready to throw you a party, Takal," Tactical said.

"So, you're saying we could be facing down the other superdreadnought in a minute or two?" Reynolds asked.

"If that," Takal answered. "The disruption is already beginning to lose its effectiveness."

"Get back on shutting them out," the AI ordered. "Ria, put some distance between us and that damn ship."

Ria jumped to follow the order, but the *Reynolds* was a brick floating in space without one of its engines.

"Do the best you can," he added. "That's all I expect."

She nodded and bent her head to her console. "I'm bringing us around to where Asya is chasing the shuttle."

Reynolds nodded and waved to Xyxl. "Do what you can to walk my engineers through increasing our shields using devium while Takal and the others work on the hacking defense."

Xyxl agreed, and Reynolds opened a channel.

"I have sent word to my crew to disable the weapon systems of the *Xzzt* so when—*if*—the ship is taken control of again, it will not be able to fire upon us immediately," the alien said.

Reynolds nodded, although he wanted to ask the alien to have his crew scuttle the superdreadnought completely. He knew that was the last ship the Gulg had in the system, outside of the stolen shuttle, and he couldn't ask them to destroy it without the means to replace it.

Which he didn't have.

"Engines are disabled on the *Xzzt* as well," Xyxl reported as he oversaw the communications with the *Reynolds'* engineering crew.

"How long will these stopgap measures work?" Maddox asked the question they all wanted to hear the answer to.

"Not long, I'm afraid," Xyxl admitted. "The enemy infiltration operates at a core level, bypassing much of the language barrier inherent in the different coding. They don't need to know the specifics of our symbology or language to instinctively do what needs to be done to operate the craft."

"That's one hell of a hack," XO whistled. "I'm just glad they haven't been able to get us with it."

"This program they're using is an AI of its own, on a much smaller scale than you," the inventor explained. "It's constantly adapting and changing, incorporating everything it encounters to better defend against attack *and* to infiltrate better.

"We got ahead of it when we dealt with the hack of Gorad's ships, but the evolution of the program is astounding." Takal shrugged. "I can't help but be impressed. This is a technological marvel."

"More of a technological nightmare since it's being used against us," Reynolds shot back. "Keep working at it,

Takal. We need that thing neutralized as soon as you can manage it."

"I'll do what I can," Takal promised, "but so you know, the disruption has ended. The *Xzzt* is once more under enemy control."

Reynolds glanced at his console and snarled. They had barely managed to inch away from the enemy ship in the time between shutting it down and now.

It wasn't remotely far enough to matter.

"Sitrep, Asya," Reynolds called over the comm.

"These guys are still dodging us," she reported back. "We were almost able to cut them off, but the damn ship is too fast for us to contain. It's also swung around the planet and entered the asteroid field, which is hampering our ability to run it down."

"We can hope it runs into a rock," Jiya suggested.

"Hope isn't a viable battle tactic," XO growled.

"No, but I'm thinking it's right up there with 'jack' and 'shit' right now," Jiya countered.

"The *Xzzt*'s engines are back up," Ria reported. "The superdreadnought is moving in our direction."

"Anything, Takal?" Reynolds asked, searching his memories for an old trick to try anew; anything that might give them an edge.

"Negative," the inventor replied.

Reynolds stared at the viewscreen, thinking and plotting. After a moment, he brought up a view of the asteroid field.

"Would we survive the asteroid field in our current condition?" the AI asked.

Jiya shook her head. "For about five minutes, before the last of our shields collapsed and we were turned to jelly."

"I'll take that as a yes," Reynolds offered as his plan started to take shape. Would five minutes be enough?

He wanted to lighten the mood because he could feel the tension in the air aboard the bridge, even though he understood how dire their situation was.

Fortunately, Takal came up with something.

"I've found another hole in the code," he announced, his voice giddy with excitement. "I'm reinforcing the shut-down commands on the weapon systems of the *Xzzt*."

"Can't you just shut the whole thing down?" Jiya asked.

The inventor shook his head. "Their people are actively working against me, in addition to the AI," he said. "I have better access to the engines and the guns because of the existing modifications we've made, but even that is difficult to maintain because they are rooting the system to plug the holes."

"What do you need?" Reynold asked.

"Time," Takal answered.

Reynolds sighed. That was the one thing they didn't have to spare. The enemy superdreadnought was closing on them.

"These bastards are good," XO told Reynolds. "I feel we will eventually overwhelm them and break the code, but it won't be soon enough to save us."

"But we're better. Never doubt that," Reynolds replied confidently.

Tactical called, "Brace for impact!"

Ria effected immediate evasive maneuvers, and the

Gulg superdreadnought hurtled past as it accelerated, strafing them from above.

It came so close to the SD *Reynolds* that it filled the viewscreen without magnification.

"Did they just try to ram us?" Jiya asked.

"They did," Ria answered. "They're coming back around for another try."

"I've cut their engines," Takal announced, "but that means they'll gain ground getting back their weapon controls."

"Should I fire on them?" Tactical asked.

Reynolds shrugged. "Not much point. Their shields are on full, and we're scraping the bottom of the barrel when it comes to power."

"The ESD is still ready, reserve power being shunted to the weapon in case we need it," Tactical advised.

"And if it fails to annihilate the ship because of the damage we've taken, we will be destroyed," Reynolds countered. "What are the odds we can get a clean hit with just one working engine?"

"Not good at all," Maddox noted. "The odds are not in our favor."

Reynolds looked back to the scanners to monitor Asya's efforts. The radiation and the asteroid field were playing havoc with his controls, and he could barely make out the shuttle and Pods in the midst of the field.

They were no closer to catching the stolen Gulg shuttle than they had been before it entered the asteroid field.

"Can you have your people shut down the ship from inside?" Reynolds asked Xyxl.

"We have been trying, doing our best to provide access

to allow for us to counter the control program, but they have had no success," the alien replied.

"Can you destroy it?" He hated asking the question, but Reynolds felt he had little choice. Something had to be done.

Xyxl shook his head. "It appears the enemy has been systematically adjusting the support systems in the ship and forcing my crew out of sensitive areas, sealing them off once they are gone. They have been unable to regain access to any part of the ship that would offer the opportunity for substantive destruction."

"Can they adjust to the atmosphere? Counter it with some kind of equipment?" Reynolds wondered as he ran through a variety of scenarios.

"They are working to do just that, but their options are limited. As you have undoubtedly noticed, my people are more an energy form than a physical one. Our needs are different from yours, and we have little use for tools since our ships are designed as an extension of our beings."

"Which means what, exactly?" Jiya asked.

"That *we* are the tools used to operate and repair the ship," Xyxl answered. "We do not rely on spare parts and extra pieces. We press our energy into the craft or that of the devium, and the ship heals. The shift in energy inside the craft is also affecting the strength of my crew, making the atmosphere toxic, but they will do what they must for as long as they are able."

As if the enemy had overhead the conversation between Reynolds and Xyxl, it ejected the remaining Gulg into space. They tumbled and spun away from the craft like tiny stars being born.

"The *Xzzt* just ejected its crew," Jiya reported.

"Damn it!" Reynolds swore. "Swing around and—"

"No need, Reynolds," Xyxl assured the AI.

A heartbeat later, the surviving Gulg appeared on the bridge of the *Reynolds*, looking frazzled. Their energy was dim.

At least they are alive, Reynolds thought.

"Damn!" Tactical exclaimed. "These assholes are cutting us off at every corner."

"I think we're going to have to ready a Gate," Reynolds admitted, although he hated to do it.

"Retreat?" Jiya asked.

Reynolds nodded. "We cannot fight this ship in our current condition, and it seems that Takal and the others will be unable to hack the cult's code before they can get their systems fully online again.

"And even if they don't get their weapons back, they've made it clear they're willing to ram us if they have to in order to take us out. We only have one ship. They have as many as they need, and we have yet to run across the *Pillar*. If that showed up right now, it would be the end of us. Standing for Justice is important, but we have to survive. There is only one of us."

"We can't leave the Muultu to the whims of the cult," Maddox said, playing devil's advocate once again.

"I don't want to," Reynolds fired back, "but I'm not seeing much of a choice here. A tactical retreat would give us time to repair the ship and work on hacking the cult's code, and allow us to come back stronger and more capable."

"It also gives them more time to get ready for us, draw

more ships to the system, and set up traps for when we return," Maddox argued. "I'm sorry, offering problems without solutions is just whining. I don't have any options for you, Captain."

"Things have just gone from bad to worse, folks," Asya announced.

"What's going on?" Reynolds asked.

"We've got incoming."

The viewscreen showed that a dozen small mining craft from Muultar were making their way toward the asteroid field. Each had the telltale gleam of the Gulg communication tether trailing behind them on the scanners.

"It's about to get real damn crowded up here," Asya muttered.

"Watch yourselves out there," he warned, knowing how unhelpful the comment was.

"ESD or bail?" Tactical asked.

"The *Xzzt*'s engines are coming back online," Ria noted. "She's on the move."

"Takal?" Reynolds called out.

"They're running us in circles," the inventor complained. "I've still got the weapons in check, but we're losing ground."

Reynolds put his hands on his hips. "Options, people."

Takal shook his head. "More time, like I said before. We need to sit down and come up with definitive counters to their moves and create some of our own. Right now we're chasing them, unable to get ahead."

Jiya cleared her throat and got everyone's attention. The silence on the bridge was deafening.

"I have an idea," she said.

CHAPTER NINETEEN

The silence remained after Jiya briefed them on what she had in mind. No one had questions. No one offered a different option.

"They're coming at us again," Ria announced as she initiated evasive maneuvers to dodge the incoming Gulg superdreadnought again. She barely managed to feint and get out of its path. The ship hurtled by, its shields rattling *Reynolds'* hull. "I don't know how many more times I'll be able to pull that off," she stated, her voice tired.

The stress was wearing on her as on everyone.

"What do we have to lose, Reynolds?" XO asked.

"Damn it," Reynolds grumbled; none of his calculations or processors could predict success. None of the options were good. If the ESD destroyed the Gulg ship but left them vulnerable, the Muultar mining ships could take the superdreadnought apart.

Jiya's idea was crazy and relied on a number of factors that couldn't be reliably controlled.

But wasn't that what combat was about?

One could only make educated guesses about what the enemy might do next. The greater the risk, the greater the reward.

Or something like that. Win the battle and end the war or run and guarantee a perpetual fight?

Reynolds didn't believe the cultists would see Jiya's plan coming.

That alone gave it a solid chance of success, all things considered. Once Reynolds decided, he was all in.

"Let do this," he commanded. "But I'm going to be the one transported across."

"Oh, hell no!" Jiya shouted. "They need you on the bridge, Captain."

"And you're flesh and blood," Reynolds countered. "If I go across and get vaporized, Takal just has to plug me into another body."

"Uh," Takal said, raising his hand, "that's not exactly true."

Reynolds spun on the man. "What do you mean?"

The inventor waved his hand, motioning from Reynolds' head to his feet. "That isn't just some shell you can pop in and out of easily. It's not that hideous Jonny-Taxi android you wore."

Takal went on, "The whole of what makes you *you* and separate from the other personalities aboard the ship is plugged into that body. I can't guarantee that your experiences and the whole of your higher functions will come back to the ship intact."

The inventor continued to talk, although he kept his

eyes on the screen in front of him, continuing his hacking battle against the cult.

"Were you to be ripped out of that body suddenly without intensive preparation ahead of time to preserve your system's integrity, as you would be if you died, it's quite possible that many of your databases would become corrupted and unreadable."

"So, you're saying I might crash?" Reynolds asked.

Takal nodded. "There is a significant risk that a catastrophic termination of this body could reboot you to a point well before you assumed this or any of the other bodies."

"Which means you're in no better position to do this than I am," Jiya crowed.

"I'm still the captain of the ship," Reynolds argued. "If I decide it's me who goes, it's me; no argument."

"Yes, sir." Jiya nodded. "So, make a decision, *Captain*. Who's it going to be?"

"Can't we just send a bot?" the AI asked Xyxl.

The alien shook his head. "Our defense systems would shut down a bot the moment it arrived. Its programming is too simplistic to avoid deactivation."

"Unlike mine." Jiya laughed, tapping the side of her head.

"But all it takes is a big thump to your head to cause a reboot of *your* system with no guarantee you'll come back," Reynolds argued.

"The *Xzzt*'s weapons are powering up," Takal warned.

"We're out of time, Reynolds," Jiya said. "You or me?"

"Me," he answered. "I can't risk losing you or any of the others. This is what it's like to be in command."

"It's my plan," she replied softly.

He shook his head, done arguing. "You have the conn, Jiya."

She took her seat in the captain's chair. "Good luck, Captain."

"Get us into position, Ensign Alcott," Reynolds ordered.

Ria did as she was told, bringing the ship about and aiming it toward the asteroid field.

The Muultu mining ships were entering the field ahead of them, closing on Asya and the two Pods Helm controlled.

"You know the drill?" Reynolds asked the pair of them over the comm.

"Yes, sir," Asya fired back.

Helm muttered something under his breath that sounded vaguely affirmative.

That was good enough for Reynolds.

"Enemy SD approaching from behind," XO noted.

"No pressure, Ensign Alcott," Reynolds started, "but please don't get us killed."

"This would be a whole lot easier if we had all our engines," she grumbled. "And maybe some time to practice."

The *Xzzt* closed as the *Reynolds* limped toward the asteroid field. The mining ships, noticing the superdreadnoughts approaching, slowed and swung around as if to impede the *Reynolds'* path into the field.

"Almost on us," Tactical announced. "Ready when you are."

"Not yet," Ria muttered under her breath.

The enemy ship drew closer and closer, filling the viewscreen.

Too late to change tack. Reynolds hovered over the controls alongside Ria in case he needed to step in.

Realistically, he knew that if he did, it wouldn't matter.

They would already be on their way to dead.

"Any time now," Tactical pressed.

Ria remained silent as the *Xzzt* sped up, scraping the SD *Reynolds'* stern. What remained of their shields flashed and shimmered when they collided.

Ria dropped the ship into a dive, shouting, "Now!"

Tactical unleashed everything he had into the face of the Gulg superdreadnought.

The viewscreen flared, adjusting to the sudden brightness, and the crew held their breaths as the *Reynolds* shuddered from the impact with the other ship and all the munitions.

And then it was over.

The *Reynolds* swooped down and around as the *Xzzt* pulled upward and away, the hulls of the two ships passing within two meters of each other.

Jiya pumped her fist. "Instinct wins every time," she shouted.

"Don't celebrate just yet," Reynolds chided.

Ria brought the *Reynolds* about, killing power to the engine and letting momentum bring them up behind the much faster Gulg superdreadnought.

The *Xzzt* slowed and came about to avoid overshooting and ending up in the asteroid field. It turned its flank to the *Reynolds* as it dodged the flurry of asteroids and aimed to come back at the *Reynolds* and try yet again to ram the ship.

"Kill the systems," Reynolds ordered.

The lights on the bridge flickered and died, emergency lighting kicking on and casting the bridge in a dull red haze. The shields dropped, not that there was much left of them, Reynolds thought, and the SD *Reynolds* floated like a derelict in space.

"Emitters charged," Tactical announced. "Firing!"

"Get out of there!" Reynolds ordered Asya and Helm.

The trio of Pods responded immediately, darting deeper into the asteroid field and shooting out above it an instant later.

The *Reynolds* trembled as if it were ready to fall apart as the bulk of its firepower was focused on the asteroid field. Just like the human game of pool, it sent a veritable planet's worth of rock into the *Xzzt*.

Ria kicked in the engine, having lured the enemy ship into thinking they were listing in space, and she steered the beam toward the fleeing spacecraft.

Its port side to them, the enemy superdreadnought did what was natural: held its course to avoid the asteroid field.

Jiya's plan, however, was not simply to blast the superdreadnought with a stern barrage, since they suspected that wouldn't be a final solution.

The weapons tore into the asteroid field, and the rocks were pulverized in their wake. Debris flew everywhere, aided by the chemical reaction of the devium present in the stone. Like supercharged electrons, pieces of asteroids scattered, setting off a chain reaction in the nearest asteroids, and then those beyond.

Within a moment, the asteroid field had become a debris field of tiny, meteors.

The *Xzzt*, while able to survive and outrun *Reynolds'* weapons, could not outrun the frenzy of the asteroid field.

Asteroids knocked loose of the field crashed into the *Xzzt's* shields like deadly hail. The shields flashed and fluttered as more and more asteroids collided with the massive ship, unable to avoid being pelted by the wreckage of the field they were skirting.

The SD *Reynolds* continued to come about, firing a second salvo of missiles.

The small mining ships joined the casualties of the asteroids, blasted to pieces. They joined the chaotic scramble of asteroids and ship pieces pelting the Gulg superdreadnought.

The last of the *Reynolds'* offensive weapons were spent. The bridge crew watched silently as the rain of asteroids continued.

The devium-accelerated rock storm continued to batter the *Xzzt* as it veered away to escape the field and reengage the *Reynolds*. Its shield lit up like the Fourth of July, debris and wreckage pounding the ship with merciless intensity.

A moment later, it cleared the wreckage and came about, shields still flickering.

"Did that work?" Reynolds asked, the entirety of the bridge holding their breaths and awaiting the answer. If the first half of the plan had worked, the second half would have to be executed with equal zeal.

Xyxl remained quiet for a moment, and it felt as if it

dragged on forever. His voice was over-loud when he finally spoke.

"Yes," was all he said.

Reynolds grinned and bared his teeth.

"Beam me up, Scotty!" he shouted.

And then he was gone.

CHAPTER TWENTY

Reynolds appeared on the bridge of the *Xzzt* and immediately began to examine himself.

A moment later, he confirmed he was still in one piece.

"Oh, thank Bethany Anne," he declared.

He hadn't believed they could pull it off, but there he was, standing on the enemy ship, staring wide-eyed at the alien technology arrayed around him.

It looked ominous in the darkness.

It took a millisecond to register that he'd actually made it, but he knew he was on the clock.

Time was running out.

"I'm in," he announced over the comm.

Muted cheers greeted him.

"Might want to hurry it up, Captain Ahab," Tactical told him. "There's a whale of a ship coming our way, and I'm all out of harpoons."

Reynolds pulled out his weapon and turned to the nearest console, unleashing a barrage of energy blasts into the stations on the Gulg superdreadnought's bridge.

Although Xyxl had told him which systems were the most valuable and vulnerable, it had been decided that strolling across the deck looking for individual consoles, especially given how alien they looked, wouldn't be an effective use of his time.

From the Pod circling above the asteroid field, Ka'nak had suggested a more effective solution, true to his nature.

"Blow it all the fuck up," the Melowi had said.

Reynolds had come there to do just that.

The AI fired energy blast after energy blast into the ship's consoles, holding his weapon in one hand and spinning in a slow circle. As he did, he tossed grenades at the farthest sections of the bridge where the resulting explosions wouldn't strike him directly.

Between lobbing grenades, he swapped power packs on his rifle and went back to work, blasting anything and everything in front of him.

"I knew I should have been the one to go," Jiya joked. "I'd have taken that thing out by now."

Reynolds kept on blasting.

As much fun as it was, the task wasn't easy. Fully powered, the Gulg ship would use its considerable resources to repair and reroute the systems he was destroying.

And while he'd believed Xyxl when he'd told him that, seeing it firsthand was something entirely different.

As if the ship were a field of weeds, the panels undulated and writhed, moving of their own volition in an effort to reconstitute themselves. The consoles shifted from side to side and inched across the deck and walls, circuits reordering and making new connections.

Within seconds, the ceiling and deck of the ship were covered in glistening vines that sparkled like living conductors.

Reynolds stared at them in amazed awe as the systems raced to stay ahead of the damage he was doing to them.

For a moment he didn't think he could keep up, but the grenades nudged the odds in his favor.

He wished he'd been able to bring a few pucks to help the process along.

He'd originally wanted to be transported to the engine room of the ship, thinking he could have taken the ship out much quicker that way, but Xyxl had convinced him not to go there.

While eliminating one of the engines would ensure that the superdreadnought was destroyed, the blast would also end up killing Reynolds, leaving him no time to escape the ship before it went up.

So there he was, raining hell down on the bridge of the Gulg SD *Xzzt* instead.

It was damn satisfying. It had been a long time since he could just cut loose and not give a shit about collateral damage.

Well, at least not directly.

The *Reynolds* was still in the path of the superdreadnought he was trying to tear up from the inside.

"Engines are flaring out," Jiya reported. "Keep going. You're doing it."

"Of course I am," he muttered, grinning while he unloaded another round into the deck and shifted across to spray the ceiling.

Takal cut in, "The code is falling apart on your end, Reynolds. I'm working to take control."

"Of what?" Reynolds asked. "There isn't anything left."

The bridge was a war zone.

The *Xzzt* had already suffered massive damage to its control systems despite its efforts to repair the harm. The ship was on a one-way trip to the junkyard.

Explosions flared around him, flames going out before they could ignite. The lack of atmosphere kept the fire in check.

Sparks danced across the ruined consoles he had shredded with his arsenal like lightning storms crackling on the horizon. The viewscreen was black and shattered, and Reynolds had no clue how close he was to his ship.

He gritted his teeth and prepared for impact every second as he continued to wreak havoc on the controls of the enemy ship.

"She's veering off," Ria shouted. "Finally."

The last was said with a breathy sigh.

More cheers sounded behind her.

"She's not quite dead yet, though," Takal warned. "Whoever's in control behind the scenes isn't giving up so easily."

"What do you mean?" Reynolds asked.

"You're passing us now, so there's no way for the ship to hurt us any longer with its weapon systems down, but they're steering it toward Muultar. I can see the AI plugging in the planet's coordinates, trying to input them before they lose control."

"Can you change its course?" Reynolds questioned.

"Working on it," was the inventor's reply, followed by a loud huff over the comm.

"I'm going to take that as a no," Reynolds said.

"The code is too fragmented now," Takal replied. "The system is too damaged to make any fine adjustments."

"Then don't even try," Reynolds told the old man. "Can you set the self-destruct?"

"Now's probably a good time to get out of there," Xyxl said over the channel. "With the ship so badly damaged, the self-destruct mechanism will take less time to arm."

"I'm ready when you are," Reynolds told the alien.

He then felt a tingle of energy pass over him, and the bridge of the Gulg ship disappeared into blackness.

Reynolds appeared on the bridge of the *Reynolds*, comforted by the sight of it.

"It's good to be home," he said, handing his weapons to Maddox. "That was fun."

He turned around and glanced at the viewscreen, seeing the *Xzzt* streaking into the blackness of space on its way toward Muultar.

And then it wasn't.

The ship went up in a sudden burst of energy, which turned into a storm of debris and glistening wreckage as the Gulg superdreadnought devoured itself.

"Pretty," Jiya said, grinning.

Reynolds turned to Xyxl. "Sorry," he told the alien. "It seems like all we do is blow up your ships, huh?"

"In this particular case, it was for the best, or all of us would be dead," he replied.

Reynolds nodded, realizing he stood alone at the front of the bridge.

"Where are all of your crew?" he asked.

"They have congregated in a room on one of the other decks," Xyxl told him. "Your people generously gave them a sanctuary where they would not have to watch the last of our ships being destroyed."

Reynolds grimaced. "You know you didn't have to stick around and watch either, right?"

Xyxl shrugged, still imitating the humanoid form. "This is my mission," he stated. "It is my place to witness its greatest and worst moments."

"Where does this one rank?" Reynolds wondered.

"Firmly at the top of the worst." He laughed. "Through no fault but my own, my mission is now concluded. We no longer have the means to carry it out."

Reynolds strode across the bridge and set a hand on the alien's shoulder. The energy tingled and ran up the AI's seemingly real arm. "That's not true. We're still here fighting against the Cult of Phraim-'Eh, and you're right here alongside us. We won't stop until this is over."

"Thank you, Reynolds," Xyxl replied, smiling.

His transparent skin made it look awkward, but Reynolds took it in the manner it was intended.

Reynolds returned to his seat after shooing Jiya out of it.

"See, I told you everything would work out fine," he told her.

Jiya laughed, shaking her head. "Yup, that's how history will tell it, too." She grabbed her own chair, plopping into it with a grunt. "The mouthy first officer was against the plan the whole time, and the heroic captain charged into the breach."

"Sounds about right," Reynolds joked, winking at Jiya.

"Too bad we're not finished," Maddox said.

Reynolds nodded. They'd managed to take out the biggest threat to them and Muultar for the moment, but the cult still rampaged across the planet, and the Gulg shuttle was still running amok.

"Anyone have eyes on that shuttle?" Reynolds asked.

"We're still chasing it, but that damn stunt with the asteroid field is making it hard as hell," Asya reported back. "We had to dodge all that debris you guys stirred up out here. It's still going, and I suspect there will be a major renovation of the entire field by the time all the energy fades."

Reynolds sighed. If they didn't catch that shuttle, he knew damn well they would end up dealing with it or the next generation of its technology. The cult surely wouldn't hesitate to put the device into action again.

"Stay on it, but watch your six," he told them, realizing he wasn't sure if they had destroyed all of the mining ships that had been launched to intercept the Pods. "We have any other ships in the area?" he asked his crew.

"One of the mining craft escaped the asteroid field, but it looks as if it's damaged. It's floundering," XO reported. "Doesn't appear to be a threat to the Pods."

"I'm more worried about us," Reynolds joked.

Kind of.

The SD *Reynolds* was so badly damaged that Reynolds worried a space wind might blow apart what was left of it, yet he had to return to Muultar and help the emperor and his council. Having abandoned the planet to return to the *Reynolds*, he wasn't sure if the emperor was still alive.

"Report," he transmitted over the comm to the Pods hovering over Ulf.

"There are some issues..." L'Eliana intoned.

CHAPTER TWENTY-ONE

Asya gritted her teeth as the Gulg shuttle pulled farther and farther ahead, shooting past the outer orbit of Muultar after having pressed hard to reach the planet once clear of the distant asteroid field.

The Pod whined as she pressed it to one hundred percent power to keep from losing the enemy ship. It didn't help that she had a full crew of people with her, including a captured empress-to-be.

Helm was doing better than she was.

The two Pods he controlled streaked ahead of her, engines flaring brightly as he too struggled to catch the quicker Gulg shuttle.

"That ship is fast and light," Helm complained over the comm. "I'm barely keeping up with it."

Asya nodded in agreement. She was able to keep tracking the stolen ship on her scanners thanks to the fact that the pilot hadn't turned off the communication tether. That not only slowed the ship down—though not by much —but it also allowed the crew to pick it up on scanners, since it essentially disabled its cloaking device with regards to them.

The shuttle circled the planet for the second time.

"I'm thinking of splitting off one of my Pods to circle back in case it comes around a third time," Helm suggested.

"I think we're better off sticking together. I don't know what else is out here. Why the hell is he circling the planet?" she asked no one in particular.

"No idea," Helm replied. "What are the odds that this ship is automated in a different way than the other Gulg ships? Maybe it's on a route."

"Who knows?" Asya replied. "With its shield and that tether on, I can't get a clear read if anyone is inside, especially not from here."

"Perhaps we should ask the alien?"

"Good idea. Hey, Xyxl," Asya called over the comm.

Comm put the alien on. "Yes?"

"Is your shuttle automated?" Asya asked.

"It can be," he answered, "but the tether must be receiving from another ship capable of controlling it, and my command ship was the only one able to do so in that manner. Well, discounting the hacked signal, of course."

"Of course." Asya sighed.

The scanners showed that the shuttle was broadcasting, not receiving, which made her think it wasn't automated at the moment.

That meant a live being was watching the systems and could see the cloaked Pods behind it just like the Gulg could. It wasn't just running to run.

There'll be no sneaking up on this guy, she thought.

But there had to be another way to get to the ship since

it continued to circle the planet as if it was waiting for something before it left the system…

Asya realized what it was doing.

"Watch out, Helm!" she shouted over the channel. "You've got incoming."

As the shuttle darted through the planet's orbit, two more of the mining craft rose out of the atmosphere and started toward Helm's Pods on attack vectors.

A third mining ship rose a few seconds later.

"He's scraping the planet for more ships to throw in our way," Asya informed Helm. "He's flying a grid around the planet, sweeping the populated areas in hopes of hooking ships he can snatch up and take over."

"I see it," Helm answered. "Tricksy bastard."

Helm initiated evasive maneuvers and dodged the lead ship, veering off at the last second and leaving the second Pod zipping in behind the first.

The pilot of the mining ship realized what he'd done at the last second, but by then it was too late.

Helm blasted the ship broadside, blowing it apart before the pilot could compensate and slip away.

The Federation Pod shot through the wreckage and burst out the other side, the glittery remains of the mining ship trailing in its wake.

Asya swooped down and launched a barrage of cannon fire at one of the mining ships, tearing up its hull and sending it tumbling into space and spilling atmosphere.

Four more ships rose from the planet as Asya shot past the last remaining one the shuttle had drawn on the last run around Muultar.

Helm circled back with his first Pod and engaged the nearest ship before it could go after Asya.

"Do these dirt-grubber ships even have weapons?" Asya asked. "I'm not seeing anything on the scanners."

"They have drilling systems, so don't let them get too close to you," the AI personality answered.

"If they're close enough to use that shit, they're close enough to ram me." Asya laughed. "I'm not playing that game with them."

Three more ships darted up from the planet as the shuttle made another pass.

"How many of these do the Muultu have?" Asya feinted right, then veered left sharply, dipping immediately after to lose one of the clumsier drilling ships.

An alert beeped in Asya's ear as the SD *Reynolds* limped into orbit around Muultar.

The Gate shimmered closed a few seconds later, and Asya swallowed hard when she saw the shape the great superdreadnought was in.

She'd known it had taken a beating but seeing it made her physically ill.

"Holy shit!" she muttered over the open channel. "You guys run face-first into a damn neutron star?"

"Feels like it," Reynolds replied. "I see you've got company."

"Yeah, that dumbass shuttle is dredging the planet for muck to throw at us," Asya remarked.

Helm double-teamed another of the mining ships, blowing it away by coming at it from both sides. It tried to dodge, but there was nowhere to go, twin Pods zipping past the exploding carcass in an X.

The Pod rattled as a mining ship collided with the back quadrant of Asya's ship.

"Son of bitch," she cursed, whipping the Pod around and chasing after the mining ship.

She blasted a hole in its stern a few moments later and sent it hurtling toward the planet's upper atmosphere, where it turned into a fireball on reentry.

"Don't get caught up with the mining ships," Reynolds warned. "You need to take that damn shuttle out or he'll just keep finding ships to throw at you."

"If I could catch the little fucker, I would," Asya argued, "but that ship is too fast for these Pods, even without a full complement of passengers."

"Another reason to be careful and not lose sight of our goal," Reynolds told her. "I don't want to lose any of you playing this cat-and-mouse game."

"Roger that!" Asya replied.

She wondered what the hell she could do to change the momentum of the chase.

As things were, they would never catch the shuttle.

"I think I've got something," Geroux called from the back, waving a small computer around.

The young tech waited until the ship leveled off, then she raced to the front and secured herself in the seat beside Asya.

"What is it?" Asya asked, barely able to give the computer more than a quick once-over.

"These guys…" she aimed a thumb at the aliens huddled in the back of the ship, "used it to send a message to a ship just like that one." She tapped the viewscreen, pointing out the elusive Gulg shuttle.

Asya shrugged, then focused on the controls as she dodged an incoming mining ship and shot past it. "And?" she asked. "What are you getting at?"

"This is tied into the same communication tether the Gulg superdreadnoughts were; the same one that shuttle is still tied into," she answered, eyebrows arched.

"You can send a message to the ship?" Asya asked, trying to figure out what Geroux was getting at.

"I can do something better," she answered.

Geroux tapped her comm and sent a request to the *Reynolds*. Takal came back a few moments later.

"Yes, child? What can I do for you?" Takal asked his niece.

"I need your and Xyxl's hacking assistance," she told him, smiling as Asya stared at her, confused.

"What do you need us to do?" the Gulg asked over the comm.

"I happen to have the computer your people gave to Aht Gow to summon your shuttle to the church," Geroux explained. "I have an idea how I can use it to catch our elusive foe, but I need some coding from you."

"Aaah," Xyxl said. "You want to use the computer to reconnect the tether, correct?"

Geroux giggled. "Exactly."

"I suppose I could download the file to you, but you have to understand that that computer is not powerful enough to take complete control over another craft. It's designed to operate in short bursts. It might be an inconvenience, little more."

"What if we tie it into the power source of the shuttle?" Geroux asked.

"You risk our stolen craft reversing your intent and taking over your ship, since his signal generator is far more powerful than yours and could easily override anything you tried to do."

Geroux sighed at hearing that, slumping into her chair and staring at the computer screen.

Asya reached over and nudged her shoulder, offering her a sympathetic smile. "It was a great idea," she said.

The young tech bolted upright, and a crooked grin flashed across her features.

"Send me the file anyway," she told Xyxl.

"As you wish," the alien replied.

There was a beep a few seconds later and Geroux's fingers played across the keyboard of the device. Asya thought the young tech looked manic as she worked, eyes gleaming.

Asya laughed. "You're scaring me."

"You're not the one who should be scared," Geroux replied with a smile. "Keep us as close to that shuttle as possible."

Asya nodded but could do nothing more than she was already doing.

Geroux hammered on the keyboard as Asya dodged the attempts by the ever-growing fleet of mining ships to ram and knock them out of space.

She and Helm took out all the ships they could, darting and weaving, then unleashing blaster fire when the opportunity presented itself.

Opportunities came more often as more ships filled the space above Muultar and pursued them. The entire time,

Geroux's keyboard clattered at Asya's side, the sound a pounding rhythm driving her on.

The shuttle veered back once more, rocketing past the Pod, and Asya got her first glance at the pilot. The scarred face of a Muultu sneered at her, and Asya saw the arrogance in his eyes when their gazes met for an instant.

Asya pulled hard to starboard and chased the shuttle.

"Motherfucker," she swore as the ship circled back and strafed her again, dodging her weapons fire easily.

The space above Muultar was starting to get crowded.

"How much longer before you're ready?" Asya asked.

She desperately wanted to blow that asshole out of the sky, especially now that he was taunting her, but she was also becoming worried about how many ships there were to contend with. Helm was trying to keep the way clear, but the coordination between the Gulg shuttle and the mining ships always resulted in the Federation Pods getting dragged into aerial killing zones.

Piloting through the cluster of mining ships was starting to get dicey.

The shuttle hurtled over them again, the pilot laughing. Asya thought she could hear him.

She realized a second later that it was Geroux she'd heard, the young girl chuckling alongside her.

"I got him," she said, amusement in her voice.

"Wait, what? How?"

Geroux grinned at Asya's confusion.

"I mixed two different programs, breeding Xyxl's remote control system with the coding that Jora'nal used to hijack Gorad's ships and the Muultu cruisers," Geroux explained.

"What will that do?"

"Watch," Geroux replied, smiling so broadly Asya feared she might split her face in two.

The shuttle darted back around, the pilot's arrogance growing

The ship flew past, dropping under the Pod this time. Asya couldn't see the pilot, but she knew he was smirking.

And then she realized he would never smirk again.

Asya burst into laughter when she saw what Geroux had done.

It wasn't the shuttle that she had tried to take over, but the low-tech mining ships the pilot had tethered to the Gulg system.

Believing himself in charge of the other craft, the pilot of the shuttle had gotten careless. He zipped by Asya's Pod and streaked into a crowd of mining ships he thought would obey his commands and move aside to let him through.

Instead, they closed ranks as he neared.

There was nowhere for him to go.

He pulled back hard on the controls, desperate to slip through the jumble of ships, but Geroux tightened the gauntlet, turning the ships in such a way that there was no room to maneuver.

"Ohhh!" Asya exclaimed when the drills flared at the moment of impact.

They sliced into the shuttle as it collided with the fleet of mining ships.

There was a fountain of sparks, and a half-dozen ships crumpled into a mangled ball of steel and tumbled end over end into the bleak emptiness of space above the planet Muultar.

Helm dropped in right behind the mess and lit it up, blowing the whole pile into so much debris.

Asya whooped and leapt out of her seat to hug Geroux.

The young tech fought to breathe, mumbling something Asya couldn't understand, pushing at her until she let go and flopped back into the pilot's seat.

"What was that?" Asya asked.

"I was telling you to watch where you were going," she said, her face pale as she struggled to catch her breath.

Asya laughed and swung the Pod around, heading back toward the *Reynolds*. "Thanks to Geroux, that wonderful Gulg technology will never grace another cultist's hands."

They could hear the grin in Reynolds' voice when he told them to, "Come on home. We've got some cultist asses to kick."

Asya had never before been so inclined to follow an order.

She grinned until the Pod docked with the superdreadnought, and probably for a while after that, too.

CHAPTER TWENTY-TWO

"Part of the city is burning," L'Eliana reported. "The tide seems to have turned, but no one is in control now. That's the big issue. It's one big stalemate."

The revolt had been an aggressive one, which was surprising, but it hadn't been an entirely effective one.

The cultists and their followers hadn't found the emperor or his council, all of them remaining safe in their hideout in the irradiated wastes that had been abandoned by even the lowest dregs of society, far from anywhere the cultists had thought to look for them.

So, the cultists had been unable to parade their captives in front of the crowd they'd tried so hard to turn against the government.

The royal guards had pulled themselves together after the initial rout and were able to maintain discipline in the face of the uprising. They lost a number of soldiers and installations, but the royal compound had been cleared of cultists and reclaimed, and several other locations had been defended. At these, the cultists and their would-be converts were made to retreat.

And since the cultists had been unable to plant a figure-head on the throne to legitimize their claim—the emperor's sister, Aht Gow, had been captive in Asya's Pod for the entirety of the attempted coup—they had also failed to win the people over with a valid successor to Krol Gow.

Reynolds flew to the emperor's hideaway in a cloaked Pod to collect him and the council and explained what had happened on the way back to the *Reynolds*. They gave the group an opportunity to clean up, eat, and catch their breath before Reynolds initiated the next move in his plan to break the last of the uprising.

"You think this is going to work?" Jiya asked the AI.

Reynolds nodded. "I had the bots do a run along the bottom of the ship and take a good look at it," he replied. "From down there, the *Reynolds* looks as it should: a vicious beast of a superdreadnought."

"Just as long as no one gets a look above that." Jiya laughed.

Reynolds sighed. "Too true."

The ship was a mess, and it would take a long time for it to be adequately cleaned up and repaired and ready for combat again.

Xyxl and his people had volunteered to help, as had the emperor, but Krol Gow's offer was more one of support rather than actual assistance.

The emperor would be too busy mending his own fences to worry about Reynolds' problems. Besides, given the disparity in the level of tech between the two societies, there wasn't much the Muultu could offer with regards to fixing up the superdreadnought.

But that was fine.

Reynolds was perfectly content to stick to the original agreement between Krol Gow and him, where the emperor provided them with a safe haven and occasional supplies when the ship wandered through the system.

Not that the SD *Reynolds* had needed much of late when it came to food or general equipment, but they would definitely need raw materials to repair the hull and reinforce the damaged portions of the ship's armor.

"You ready?" Jiya asked.

Reynolds nodded. "Yeah, let's get everyone and go save the day." He turned to Asya, pointing at the captain's chair. "You've got the conn, Captain."

She saluted him and took the seat. "This is going to be interesting."

"Shock and awe!" Tactical crowed.

"Let us know when we've arrived," Reynolds told Asya as he and Jiya marched off the bridge to meet the rest of the folks who would be joining them.

The *Reynolds* broke orbit and plunged through the atmosphere of Muultar. The ship rattled as it descended, and Reynold worried it would fall apart before they arrived. All his plans would be scrapped if an engine fell off during their descent.

He chuckled at that thought, and Jiya caught him. He cast a smile her way.

"What are you so happy about?" she asked as they wound through the wide corridors of the ship.

"Despite everything that happened, we learned a lot about our enemy on this mission, and while it's not quite over, I expect we'll learn far more once we get a chance to sit down and have a real discussion with Xyxl and his people, not to mention the emperor's sister."

Jiya nodded her understanding.

"Now all we have to do is quell a rebellion, then we'll be able to get to work on the ship. Maybe just this once we'll be able to get ahead of Jora'nal and that bastard Phraim-'Eh, whoever he is."

After that, the pair walked in companionable silence until they reached the chambers within the superdreadnought where the emperor, his council, and his sister had been quartered.

Reynolds had set guards on the door and left Ka'nak in the room to contain Aht Gow in case she got rambunctious. However, she'd been a model prisoner since she had learned that her precious cult had been all but wiped out and the leaders she'd believed were true members turned out to be alien imposters.

It probably helped that Krol Gow had threatened to throw her into space for daring to try to usurp his throne.

Reynolds had escorted them both to the hangar bay and had shown the emperor how the airlocks worked. Aht Gow spent a few eternal hours locked in the airlock's decompression chamber, fearful that the glowing green light would go out and be replaced by the crimson glow that would see her ejected into the cold of space.

Aht Gow stared at the floor as Reynolds and Jiya came into the room.

"Emperor," Reynolds greeted him, giving the monarch a shallow nod.

Krol Gow returned the greeting, smiling at Jiya. The council was quiet, but they offered their own greetings. Aht Gow, of course, said nothing.

Jiya smiled and waved at Ka'nak, who raised an eyebrow and pointed with his eyes at the emperor's sister. He stuck his tongue out, and Jiya stifled a laugh.

"Are you ready to reclaim your empire?" Reynolds asked, ignoring his crew's antics.

"Indeed," Krol Gow answered, "although I don't feel as if I lost it, thanks to you and your people. We will need to discuss my gratitude once all this is behind us."

Reynolds dismissed the idea. "We need very little from you, Emperor, yet we can offer you much to show our friendship."

"You have done that and more already." Emperor Krol Gow smiled.

He paused a moment, his pleasant expression turning darker. Maudlin, almost.

"Do you believe that this will work?"

"Only one way to find out," Reynolds replied. "Let's get this show on the road. Or on the hull, as it were."

"We've touched down," Asya reported over the ship-wide comm.

Reynolds waved for the emperor and his people to follow him and Jiya. The council walked at their backs. Ka'nak escorted Aht Gow, and although he didn't touch her, she flinched every time the Melowi warrior got too close.

The group made their way down the hall to a hatch that led out onto the hull of the ship. Bots opened the hatch as they approached, and fresh air spilled into the *Reynolds* along with murmured chatter from below.

Reynolds stepped out on the wide platform of the ship, urging the others on. They gathered outside after a moment, the royals doing their best to maintain their appearance of regality. Reynolds knew they were afraid of the height and the exposure.

Asya had brought the superdreadnought down so that it hovered above the city of Ulf, a great monster in the sky above the swirling chaos of the uprising.

The crowd stilled as the ship loomed and Tactical ignited the ESD, charging the system. Impressive arcs of lightning played across the barrel of the massive weapon, and it was only the sudden burst of loudspeaker static that kept the crowd from fleeing for their lives.

They stood frozen in terror, having never before seen a steel behemoth such as the *Reynolds* dominating their city.

The AI Reynolds stepped out where he could be seen and raised his hands to the crowd, the ship's system magnifying his voice while the ship magnified his presence.

"I am Captain Reynolds of the Federation Superdreadnought *Reynolds*," he announced.

There was absolute silence in the wake of his announcement.

"I stand before you today to declare that the Cult of Phraim-'Eh is no more."

Murmurs washed over the crowd.

"We have conquered them here on Muultar and

beyond, and we warn you now," he went on, not caring that he was exaggerating or straight-up lying to the people. He needed them scared and compliant. He needed them to listen. "You have been lied to by Phraim-'Eh and his minions. He is no god, and he is no savior. He is a being just like us."

The crowd shuffled around as Reynolds spoke.

"Let it be known that we protect the emperor against all enemies."

Reynolds waved the emperor forward, and Krol Gow came to the edge of the ship where he could be seen. His council slowly came up behind him.

"Emperor Krol Gow is alive and well, and he is still in command of Ulf and the Empire of Muultar." The AI gestured to the monarch, who waved in response. "The ruling council remains in place, unharmed."

Ripples of surprise spilled through the throng at seeing their leaders hovering above them upon the machine of death.

Ka'nak nudged Aht Gow forward, staying close enough to ensure that she could be seen but couldn't do anything stupid like jump into the crowd.

"The rebellion stirred up by Phraim-'Eh is no more!" Reynolds said again, motioning so that everyone got a good look at Aht Gow and the shame on her face. "We will not tolerate another attempt," Reynolds warned.

As agreed upon before they had gone outside, Reynolds stepped back and let the emperor speak.

"I understand the desperation and fear that drove you to do what you did, and I forgive you, since the circumstances that led to this unfortunate situation were manufactured by the Cult of Phraim-'Eh. They were behind our shortage of devium and behind the darkness that has crept into our lives. You have my word that neither will hold sway over us any longer."

The crowd was slow to respond, but then cheers went up in waves, the various sections of the throng joining in until the whole raised their voices as one.

The emperor waited until the noise abated before continuing.

"If you had any part in this attempted rebellion, I ask that you return home to your families and never speak of this again. Never speak of this horrid cult or Phraim-'Eh ever again." He leaned out and met the eyes of the crowd. "Those who stand down and walk away will be allowed to return to their lives as though this never happened. We will move forward from this day on, and we will do it together!"

The crowd roared their approval, and although they couldn't see what was going on around them, Reynolds spied the soldiers slipping unnoticed through the assemblage.

The rank and file citizen who'd gotten caught up in the frenzy and fear would be left to go about their lives. The true cultists, however, would be rounded up and imprisoned, and Reynolds would get his turn at questioning them in the hopes that they would divulge everything they knew about Jora'nal and the cult.

"Now, return to your homes, comforted by the fact that we have new allies with much to share with us and that our source of devium is accessible to us once more. Ulf and the whole of Muultar will prosper!"

The emperor raised his hands, and the crowd cheered until the soldiers tactfully began to nudge people on their way.

As the crowd slowly dispersed, Reynolds and the council went back inside, the bots sealing the door behind them with a loud *thump*.

Reynolds turned to the emperor, who looked pale but stood tall in the glow of his triumphant return to power.

"I cannot thank you enough, Reynolds," Krol Gow said.

The AI smiled. "We will sit and talk soon, Emperor, but now I need to concentrate on repairing my ship." The two shook hands, and the AI gestured to Jiya when they broke apart. "My first officer here will return you and your people to your compound, and we are only a call away should you need us."

Both sides said their thanks and goodbyes, and Jiya escorted them off the ship and back to the royal compound.

Once she returned, the SD *Reynolds* launched into an orbit around the planet, settling in for a long stay.

There was much to be done, and much to be learned.

Xyxl had promised to share the technology of their instant transportation system in exchange for the entirety of the code that would keep the cult from invading the Gulg systems again, as well as a ride back to their home planet once everything was said and done.

Reynolds thought that was a damn good deal.

He could only imagine the things he could accomplish

with an ally like the Gulg in the fight against this new generation of Kurtherian threat.

Together, he and his crew would bring the war to Jora'nal and Phraim-'Eh and destroy the cult that had plagued them since he had begun his mission, which had since become about eliminating the cult and all that it represented regarding Kurtherians long gone.

Bethany Anne would be proud, he believed.

CHAPTER TWENTY-THREE

The Voice of Phraim-'Eh stood at the back of the cathedral staring down the long, red-carpeted aisle that led to his master.

He regretted the news he had to share.

Members of the church sat in the pews and stared at the master as he perched upon his throne, praying to him with every ounce of devotion they could muster. Murmured praises filled the air as the Voice swallowed the knot in his throat and started down the aisle.

His master did not reward cowardice, only obedience.

The crowd's heads were bowed in reverence, so no one noticed that the Voice walked among them.

He was grateful, because now was not the time for the people to rise up and beg to hear the voice of their god. No, there would be only regret and recrimination in such words, and the Voice could not bring himself to speak such before his lord.

As he strode forward, he felt the eyes of his master fall

upon him, a weight as if a tomb door had closed at his back.

The Voice knew fear then. Abject terror, but still his feet stroked the blood-red carpet as he approached the dais where his master sat. He marched forward without slowing.

He could feel his heart thundering in his chest, his life's blood scalding his veins under the gaze of his god.

Then, before he could think to draw a breath, the Voice stood before the steps of the dais. The quiet prayers of obeisance behind him faded into silence; the Voice had ears for no one but his lord.

The barest whisper of a wave summoned him.

He made his way up the steps of the low dais and prostrated himself at the feet of his master, but he knew better than to beg forgiveness or spit subservient words to no purpose other than to spare himself his god's wrath.

"My lord, I have failed," he said plainly, not mincing his words. "The mission on Muultar has failed, and we have lost the planet and the system's resources."

Phraim-'Eh sat back, his throne creaking under the weight of his fury.

"The Federation AI Reynolds found his way to the planet and interfered with our plans, forcing us to enact them before we were ready. We no longer have a foothold there, and the minion of Bethany Anne remains behind to spread the word of her Federation."

A wave of fetid heat washed over the Voice as his master snarled his disappointment. The Voice blinked away the moist warmth that pecked at his eyes, but he kept his gaze firmly planted on the floor at his master's feet.

He dared not raise his head and meet his lord's naked rage.

There was a moment of silence as the Voice waited for the condemnation of his deity, each passing second an agonizing eternity as he waited to be struck down, but no blow came.

He waited in terror a moment longer, then he found his voice once more. He swallowed hard so that his words did not tremble as they fell from his tongue and asked, "What would you have me do, Master?"

Phraim-'Eh rose from his chair and stood before the Voice, the ground trembling beneath him.

There was a sharp clap above him, and the world stilled in its wake. Pressure coalesced an instant later, and hell seemed to rise into the room.

He screamed as he felt his blood boil and his eyes pressed hard against their lids, desperate to escape their sockets.

Then he heard a storm.

Where there had been silence, there was now a maelstrom. Where there had been prayers, he heard shrieks.

Thunder rumbled all around, and the Voice could smell fire and sulfur and taste the coppery tang of blood and ash upon his tongue.

He resisted the urge to curl into a fetal position and beg the forgiveness of his lord. Instead, he held strong against the coming apocalypse, his ears ringing from the harpy shrieks of wind and his bones rattling in his flesh.

When it seemed he could no longer stand it, that he would bleed out his very essence and be left a pool at the feet of his deity, silence returned.

A breeze washed over him, and he felt warm rain patter on his cheeks and forehead.

A powerful hand settled beneath his chin and raised him to his feet.

The Voice screamed inside; begged himself to keep his eyes closed and remain strong in the face of his god, but a single word drilled into his skull.

"Look."

The Voice's eyes flew open, and he beheld his god.

Phraim-'Eh was crimson of skin, and gleaming obsidian eyes sat above the ledges of his cheekbones, which looked to be carved from granite. Long dark hair waved gently in the breeze, and the Voice could feel the power emanating through the palm of his master's hand as it held him aloft.

Phraim-'Eh adjusted his grip so the Voice could stare into the endless wells that were his eyes, and the Voice felt his sanity slipping away.

"Do nothing," Phraim-'Eh told him, his voice a whisper and the roar of an erupting volcano all at once. "I will handle this Reynolds myself."

Phraim-'Eh released the Voice and he tumbled to his knees, not feeling the cold granite as his bones ground into the stone.

His eyes shut of their own accord, and by the time he could force them open again, his lord was gone.

He knew not how long it had been since he'd entered the cathedral or how long he'd spent on his knees in supplication, but now it was time to gather himself and be away until his master called upon him again.

The Voice rose on shaky legs. He turned, his mind in a blur, and staggered down the steps.

The whole of the cathedral had been wiped from existence.

Where pews and stone walls and arched ceilings and people had been, now there was nothing but dust and the constant patter of the rain that fell from above in warm spatters.

It wasn't until the Voice was nearly free of the cathedral's ruin that he realized the rain was blood.

The End

Don't stop now! Keep turning the pages as Craig talks about his thoughts on this book and the overall project called the Age of Expansion.

AUTHOR NOTES - CRAIG MARTELLE

JANUARY 29, 2019

Thank you for reading this book, and you're still reading! Oorah, hard-chargers. I really hope you liked this story.

We will have one more *Superdreadnought* to wrap the series and then we'll be off to tell the next story. I had originally planned for eight books, but plans change as a series unfolds. These are different stories than what people were expecting—it is space opera and character driven. I know that a vocal group wanted more of Reynolds kicking ass and less living-creature interference, but I wanted a *Star Trek the Original Series* vibe. I think we got that, and it resonated from that perspective.

It's all good—a story to entertain, as the next will, but

even better:) We try to get better with each new word, new sentence, and new story.

Metal Legion is destroying its opponents. I am pleased with how that series is running away with the readers. We're bringing more and more on board with each new volume. And we're growing the world – in the *Metal Legion* universe, you're going to see *Battleship Leviathan*. That series will take the lessons we learned from *Superdreadnought* and the good feedback from *Metal Legion* and deliver a hard-hitting, great-reading series about space battles and one ship against many.

I look forward to delivering the new series and enjoying your reaction. It is going to be exceptional.

Here in the sub-Arctic, we're in the throes of the cold/hot exchange. It went from -40F to +25F in the course of three days. I'm good with the +25, especially since that is Phyllis the Arctic Dog's favorite temperature. She is a pit bull, but her hair is as thick as a sea otter's (Darwin's evolution in a couple years living in the Arctic within a single generation). At 50F she starts to pant heavily. We get outside as much as possible when it's this warm in the winter. We'll go six months without temperatures getting above freezing, so any days in the 20s are bonus days and shorten the winter considerably.

I'm home for a while. My next trip will be to Lake Geneva, Wisconsin for GaryCon XI – a convention in honor of Gary Gygax and his invention, *Dungeons and Dragons*. It's a total bash as we play games and BS for four days straight. We eat way too much at the buffet, but it's only once a year:) This will be my third in a row. I caught the flu last year, but I have high hopes of staying healthy this time around.

I hope the Arctic blast in the Lower 48 that's ongoing right now doesn't hurt anyone. My brother (lives in Illinois) told me that he spent two hours plowing half a foot of snow from his long-ass driveway and big parking area and that wind chill was -50F the entire time. It did a number on his truck's plow hydraulics. Have to wait for it to warm up to fix it, just like I had to with my tractor. I blew the snow-blower belt and had to wait for all the snow to melt off of it before I could put on the new belt. I was victorious, despite the mean machine trying to rip skin off my knuckles. I'll take it for a test drive today to make sure everything is working. But I have a heated garage and that's what it takes to work on my tractor. We're on a first-name basis because of how much time we've spent together, my tractor and me.

That's it – I have *Superdreadnought 5*'s outline to dig into. and then the final draft of *Mystically Engineered 2* to review and get to the editor.

Peace, fellow humans.

Please join my Newsletter (www.craigmartelle.com – please, please, please sign up!), or you can follow me on Facebook since you'll get the same opportunity to pick up the books for only 99 cents on that first Saturday after they are published.

If you liked this story, you might like some of my other books. You can join my mailing list by dropping by my website www.craigmartelle.com, or if you have any comments, shoot me a note at craig@craigmartelle.com. I am always happy to hear from people who've read my work. I try to answer every email I receive.

If you liked the story, please write a short review for me on Amazon. I greatly appreciate any kind words. Even one or two sentences go a long way. The number of reviews an ebook receives greatly improves how well it does on Amazon.

Amazon – www.amazon.com/author/craigmartelle

BookBub – https://www.bookbub.com/authors/craig-martelle

Facebook – www.facebook.com/authorcraigmartelle

My web page – www.craigmartelle.com

That's it—break's over, back to writing the next book. Peace, fellow humans.

Craig Martelle's other books (listed by series)

Terry Henry Walton Chronicles (co-written with Michael Anderle) – a post-apocalyptic paranormal adventure

Gateway to the Universe (co-written with Justin Sloan & Michael Anderle) – this book transitions the characters from the Terry Henry Walton Chronicles to The Bad Company

The Bad Company (co-written with Michael Anderle) – a military science fiction space opera

End Times Alaska (also available in audio) – a Permuted Press publication – a post-apocalyptic survivalist adventure

The Free Trader – a Young Adult Science Fiction Action Adventure

Cygnus Space Opera – A Young Adult Space Opera (set in the Free Trader universe)

Darklanding (co-written with Scott Moon) – a Space Western

Rick Banik – Spy & Terrorism Action Adventure

Become a Successful Indie Author – a non-fiction work

Enemy of my Enemy (co-written with Tim Marquitz) – a galactic alien military space opera

Superdreadnought (co-written with Tim Marquitz) – a military space opera

Metal Legion (co-written with Caleb Wachter) - a military space opera

End Days (co-written with E.E. Isherwood) – a post-apocalyptic adventure

Mystically Engineered (co-written with Valerie Emerson) – dragons in space (coming Jan 2019)

Monster Case Files (co-written with Kathryn Hearst) – a young-adult cozy mystery series (coming Mar 2019)

For a complete list of books from Craig, please see www. craigmartelle.com